I0600710

IMPORTANT BILLING AND CREDIT REQUIREMENTS

CONTENTS

To Dan Lauria
for the inspiration ...

To Joe Cacaci
for his dedication ...

... and to all the rest of my "goombata"
at PKE for their perspiration ...

... these plays are lovingly dedicated.

MEN IN SUITS

THREE PLAYS ABOUT THE MAFIA

by

Jason Milligan

A SAMUEL FRENCH ACTING EDITION

SAMUEL FRENCH

FOUNDED 1830

New York Hollywood London Toronto

SAMUELFRENCH.COM

ISBN 978-0-573-62628-9   Printed in U.S.A.   #21983

MEN IN SUITS

CHARACTERS

MAX
BOBBY
THE BOSS

SETTING

Various locations in New York, on Long Island, and on the road to Vermont. All of these locations are suggested with a set piece or two— a bench for Grand Central Station, two stools for the car, a table and chairs for IHOP, etc.

Light and sound will play an important role in establishing all of these locations.

MEN IN SUITS was originally presented as a staged reading at the Westwood Playhouse in Los Angeles in November, 1991 under the auspices of the Patchett Kaufman Entertainment Theatre play reading series with the following cast:

Bobby ....RON PERLMAN
Max ....DAN LAURIA
The Boss ....PETER FALK

MEN IN SUITS received its world premiere at the Westport Country Playhouse in Westport, Connecticut on August 5, 1996 under the direction of Joe Cacaci. The cast was as follows:

Bobby ....DAN LAURIA
Max ....JAMES HANDY
The Boss ....CHARLES DURNING

The scenic and projection design were by Richard Ellis, the costumes were designed by Kathryn Morrison, lighting was designed by Susan Roth, sound was designed by Charles Dayton, the production stage manager was Neil Krasnow, the advance stage manager was Ruth Moe and the assistant to the director was Maura McGuinness.

The play was co-produced by Ted Weiant in association with The Playwrights' Kitchen Ensemble, Richard Zavaglia, co-artistic director, and by special arrangement with Buncha Guys Productions.

ACT I

Scene 1

(SETTING: Grand Central Station, New York. In total darkness, we hear a train pulling into the station. Its brakes squeal their high-pitched, piercing whine as the train slows. The sound of the brakes' squeal begins to change, and we realize we are listening to a person screaming. The scream fades out completely as lights come up on MAX and BOBBY, seated on a bench in the waiting area of Grand Central Station. Train station sounds [announcements, et al] play faintly in the background throughout the scene.
AT RISE: BOBBY and MAX wear nice suits and look like stockbrokers. A briefcase sits on the floor, leaned against MAX's end of the bench. BOBBY holds a folded-up copy of the New York Post, which he fiddles with nervously. MAX writes intently on a yellow legal pad. Establish this, then:)

BOBBY. Hey, Max?

MAX. (Busy writing:) Yeah ...?

BOBBY. You remember that guy?

MAX. What guy?

BOBBY. In Boston. (MAX looks at BOBBY, doesn't respond, returns to his writing.) You know. That *guy*. In *Boston*!

MAX. What are you talking about?

BOBBY. You 'member that time we went to Boston? Yeah you do. That *guy*! Remember? We went on the train, you and me. Remember? In South Station? In the bathroom.

MAX. Oh ...

BOBBY. Yeah.

(Beat.)

MAX. Well?

BOBBY. What?

MAX. What about him?

7

BOBBY. I dunno, I's just sittin' here, thinkin' about him.

MAX. Why?

BOBBY. Huh?

MAX. Why were you thinking about him *now*?

BOBBY. I dunno. I guess ... I guess this kinda reminds me of Boston.

MAX. This ain't Boston.

BOBBY. I know it ain't Boston. Ha! Boston ... It's Grand Central Station. But here we are, you know, sittin' here waiting for some *guy* ... kinda like in Boston. *(Beat.)* Except in Boston, we stabbed that guy while he was takin' a crap. I hope we don't have to do *that* again.

MAX. Oh, all of a sudden you're squeamish, is that it?

BOBBY. Oh, no. No. It was just so ...

(Long pause as BOBBY searches for the proper word. MAX gets tired of waiting.)

MAX. So ... what?

BOBBY. *(He's got it:)* Disrespectful.

MAX. Disrespectful?

BOBBY. Yeah. Of a human bean. To stab him while he's takin' a crap. Crappin' is a very private thing, you know. More private than sex or somethin'. I can't stand havin' anybody watchin' me. And there we were, *stabbin'* him! *(Beat.)* You 'member Virginia?

MAX. Who?

BOBBY. That girl. That woman I was seein'. You remember. She and me was—

MAX. Oh, yeah.

BOBBY. Yeah. Well, that's why she had them two false teeth.

MAX. I didn't know she had any false teeth.

BOBBY. Yeah. She did. Over on the side—

(BOBBY indicates where.)

MAX. Those were false teeth?

BOBBY. Yeah.

MAX. They looked real to me.

BOBBY. I know, they did a good job.

MAX. Why'd she have two false teeth?

BOBBY. Because. I knocked the real ones *out*!

MAX. *You* did?

BOBBY. Yeah.

MAX. You never told me that!

BOBBY. I'm tellin' you *now*! That's the *reason* I knocked 'em out. She was tryin' to watch me while I was takin' a crap one night!

MAX. Why would she wanna see that?

BOBBY. Beats the hell outta me. I'm not much to look at, even in a $1,200 suit, I'm sure I'm a helluva lot *less* to look at with my pants down around my ankles, flippin' through *People* magazine.

MAX. I don't wanna hear what you read when you're on the toilet!

BOBBY. I don't really *read* it; just look at the pictures. You know. Who's datin' who—

MAX. Why are you telling me all this?

BOBBY. Cause. I'm *sayin'*— *(Beat; what was he saying? Oh, yeah:)* That I hope we don't do this guy on the toilet. That's all I'm sayin'.

MAX. Well, we're not.

BOBBY. Good.

MAX. We're doing him at a pay phone.

BOBBY. Yeah?

MAX. Boss says he'll get off the 9:22 and go straight to the pay phones over there. Always does. Every Friday. He'll dial a number and he'll talk to somebody—we don't know who—for about a half a minute. Then he'll hang up and go out to the street and flag a taxi.

BOBBY. Except ...

MAX. Yeah?

BOBBY. Tonight ...?

MAX. Yeah ... ?

BOBBY. *(Chuckling:)* ... he ain't gonna be takin' no taxi!

MAX. *(Same:)* No ...

BOBBY. *(Greatly relieved.)* Whew. Well, *that's* good. I feel a *lot* better now. I'd *much* rather stick some guy at a pay phone than on the john. That's a lot better, don't you think? I think so. *(Beat.)* Don't you think?

MAX. Bobby?

BOBBY. Yeah?

MAX. Quit *talking* so much! You always start talking like some kinda parrot or something whenever we gotta do somebody.

BOBBY. No I don't! I do *not*! Talk? Me. Like I *talk* a lot. What about *you*? Huh? You talk plenty. You talk—I may talk, but you! Man. *(Beat.)* Except lately. You been mighty quiet lately ... *(Beat; BOBBY looks around.)* Maybe I'm just a little nervous, okay? Maybe—well, if *you* hadda be the one to *stab* a guy, you'd—I mean, all you gotta do is talk to the Boss and set everything up! I'm the one who's gotta—Do you ever stop and think—? I mean, you know. C'mon Max!

MAX. I'm sorry, Bobby.

BOBBY. I know, I know. Well ... s'my job, I guess. I oughtta just stop complainin', huh?

MAX. Well ...

BOBBY. Tony D'Angelino says it's like the Boy Scouts.

MAX. What is?

BOBBY. *This.*

MAX. Tony D'Angelino?

BOBBY. Yeah.

MAX. Is he the one with the gold teeth?

BOBBY. Yeah! That's him!

MAX. He's an idiot.

BOBBY. No, but he says, the Boss notices things. Appreciates things. Rewards people for things. He was telling me, like, not to complain so much. He says you go right on, you stick enough guys in pay toilets, one a these days you'll get moved up a notch. I could. Maybe. Like you. You used to be a low man on the totem pole and now look at you. *(MAX looks at him.)* Well, you know. You get moved up a notch ... *I* get moved up a notch ... that's how it works. Leapfrog.

MAX. "Leapfrog?"

BOBBY. Yeah. You know ... *(BOBBY makes a motion with his hands, one hand jumping over the other. MAX shakes his head, returns to his writing.)* Tony D'Angelino was saying how it's like the Boy Scouts. Cause in the Boy Scouts you win them Merit Badges and earn your way up in the ranks. That's kinda like what we're doin'. We're earnin' our way up the ranks. I mean, think about it, Max. You could be the Boss one a these days! *(MAX waves this off as a silly notion.)* You could! And then, I could take your spot! If the Boss sees I got initiative ... he could move me up a notch or two.

MAX. He won't.

BOBBY. He might.

MAX. He won't.

BOBBY. Why not?

MAX. Because.

BOBBY. 'Cause what?

MAX. You *talk* too much!

(Long pause.)

BOBBY. What are you writing anyway? Two weeks now, I'm the one doing all the talking and you just sit there, scribbling away like that court stenographer out at Brooklyn Circuit Court. You remember her?

MAX. Yeah ...

BOBBY. She didn't have no legs. Remember? She sat in that motorized wheelchair—

(BOBBY imitates the noise.)

MAX. Yeah ...

BOBBY. But, man, could she *type*! I was cussin' at that Judge, a mile a minute, and she was gettin' it all down in her little typewritin' machine thing. *(Beat.)* What are you writing, Max?

MAX. A letter to my mother.

BOBBY. No, I'm serious. What are you writing?

(Before MAX can answer, we hear the sound of a train pulling out of the station. MAX looks up, is about to address BOBBY, when something in the distance catches his eye. The departing train's horn blows.)

MAX. Here he comes.

(BOBBY looks up. They both stand in unison now, facing in the direction of their unseen victim. A knife flashes open in BOBBY's hand. The train's horn becomes a person's scream. Blackout.)

Scene 2

(SETTING: The scream continues in the black, then fades as lights come up on MAX's place on Long Island. An hour later. MAX stands as BOBBY paces feverishly. Something went wrong ...)

BOBBY. Dammit ...

MAX. Don't panic.

BOBBY. ... Dammit! Dammit! Dammit!

MAX. It's not the end of the world, Bobby.

BOBBY. Yeah, right ...

MAX. It's *not*!

BOBBY. You stand there and say that. Stand there. I mean. Easy for *you* to say!

MAX. Okay. So you stuck the wrong guy; big *deal*.

BOBBY. It *is* a big deal, Max! He's *dead*! *(Beat.)* You know how things are. I mean. Okay. When something goes wrong, who always gets their balls cut off?

MAX. What are you talking about—?

BOBBY. Traditionally. Who always gets castrated when there's a screw-up?

MAX. Bobby, we've never screwed-up before—

BOBBY. I'm not talking about *us*. I'm talking about, you know. In General.

MAX. I dunno ...

BOBBY. Theoretical.

MAX. I *dunno*!

BOBBY. The Guy on the Bottom, Max. The Fella at the Bottom of the Totem Pole always gets crucified. That's *me*, Max. I'm the guy at the "bottom."

MAX. You're not, Bobby!

BOBBY. I am, Max! I'm the one at the bottom and you're one step on top a me!

MAX. Look. If it makes you feel any better, *I* was the one, told you to stick the guy.

BOBBY. Yeah ...

MAX. So, if the Boss is gonna be mad at anybody, he's probably gonna be mad at *me*.

BOBBY. I dunno ...

MAX. Trust me.

BOBBY. You said—You said the Boss told you to look for this guy—Waspy guy, you read me the description—comin' off the 9:22 from—

MAX. Katonah—

BOBBY. —Katonah, wearin' a suit, goin' to the pay phone—

MAX. Right ...

BOBBY. —and this guy looked exactly like that and so I did exactly that!

MAX. So?

BOBBY.	MAX.
Max, if you hadn't a snatched his wallet and we hadn't a looked inside, we never woulda known he was—	How many times do I hafta say it? I was the one who told you to stick him! How was I to know it was—

BOBBY & MAX. *(In unison.)* —THE WRONG GUY!!

MAX. BOBBY, LISTEN TO ME, —I *TOLD* YOU TO DO IT!!

BOBBY. THAT DON'T MAKE NO DIFFERENCE! Cause: the right guy is out there someplace, eatin' a slice a pizza or doin' some girl right now and the Boss is gonna be mad as hell when he finds out!

You know how he is, Max. You seen what happens when he gets pissed. *(Beat.)* What do you think he's gonna do?

MAX. Who?

BOBBY. The Boss.

MAX. Bobby—

BOBBY. You 'member that time he sent Little Joey Carmello down to Nick's Candy Store to pick up Nick's payment?

MAX. That was entirely different—

BOBBY. *(Topping him:)* —Nick was, like, two months overdue on his payments and the Boss told Joey Carmello to make sure he got the money. It was, like, this "test" for Joey. So Joey Carmello goes down there, picks up the package ... and he comes back to the Boss with this brown paper bag. Smilin'—you 'member how cocky he was—he tosses it right down on the Boss's desk and he says. "I got it." And you 'member how the Boss opened the bag and reached down in there to get the cash—

MAX. Bobby—

BOBBY. —and he sticks his hand—

MAX. *(He's heard this legend a million times:)* —into a bunch of cat shit, yeah, yeah.

BOBBY. And there's Little Joey Carmello standing there, still smilin' like some dumb son of a bitch, he doesn't even *realize*—and instead of going back to Nick's Candy Shop and doin' something awful to Nick, who was the guy who *put* the cat shit in the bag, the Boss decides to make an example out of Joey Carmello and so he—

BOBBY and MAX. *(Simultaneous:)* —breaks nine of Little Joey's fingers!

BOBBY. —crushes 'em! Every one except the left pinky finger!

MAX. Bobby. The Boss ain't gonna crush your fingers—

BOBBY. *(Examining his hand and pondering his fate:)* It'd be awful hard to tie a tie without my fingers, wouldn't it? Awful hard to do a lotta things ...

MAX. Bobby. The Boss is not going to break your fingers.

BOBBY. How do you know?

MAX. I just—I *know*, okay?

BOBBY. Not really. You just *think* you know.

MAX. Yeah, well, maybe I *think* I know the Boss a little bit better than you.

BOBBY. *(Terrified:)* He's gonna be furious ...

MAX. It was an *honest mistake*!

BOBBY. *(Picks up the phone and offers it:)* You could call him!

MAX. Who?

BOBBY. The Boss.

MAX. Why?

BOBBY. Call him up and tell him that things went sour.

MAX. What, are you *crazy*? I'm not calling the Boss! On a Friday night at 11:00? He'd *kill* me if I got him outta bed!

BOBBY. See? You're scared of him too!

MAX. No I'm not!

BOBBY. NINE BROKEN FINGERS!!

MAX. Bobby! Bobby, look. Look! We can't call him and wake him up. He'll be mad as hell. I mean, you know. It's Friday night; the Boss goes to bed early ... okay? But. Tomorrow morning, bright and early, he'll wake up, he'll have his breakfast in bed and his boys'll come in and they'll catch him up to date on things while he eats his grapefruit. He'll find out that we made a mistake ... and it'll be a fresh new day and he'll be happy to see the sunshine and just be sitting there eating his grapefruit ... and he'll give us a second chance.

BOBBY. Max.

MAX. Yeah.

BOBBY. You ever *see* the Boss first thing in the morning?

MAX. *(Not really:)* Well ...

BOBBY. First thing in the morning. When he first wakes up.

MAX. I—

BOBBY. I mean, *right* when he wakes up. Before he takes a leak.

MAX. Ah ... no.

BOBBY. I didn't think so.

MAX. Why?

BOBBY. Max ... he don't eat grapefruit; they say he eats *people* for breakfast.

MAX. What?

BOBBY. Tony D'Angelino says he has to have six, seven tranquilizers with his tomato juice.

MAX. Nah ...

BOBBY. And three shots of vodka!

MAX. What?

BOBBY. Billy the Moose says he's a raving maniac when he gets up! So just *think* how awful it's gonna be if he wakes up to *bad news*!

(Beat.)

MAX. Okay, then. So what're we gonna do? You got any ideas?

BOBBY. Yeah. I do.

MAX. Shoot.

BOBBY. Let's go see him.

MAX. What?

BOBBY. Yeah.
MAX. The *Boss*?
BOBBY. Why not?
MAX. In *Vermont*?
BOBBY. What, is that where he lives?
MAX. Yeah.
BOBBY. Okay, then. In Vermont.
MAX. Bobby, I am *not* showing up on the Boss's doorstep with bad news. I'm just not.
BOBBY. Then *I'll* do it.

(BOBBY starts for the door.)

MAX. Bobby—
BOBBY. Max, it's our only hope! If he wakes up and those bums tell him that Bobby and Max screwed up a hit and they all sit around and talk about it and talk about it and make it sound worse and worse and worse ... he's just gonna get madder and madder until his *veins* stand out on his head! *But*—if we're *there*, right when he wakes up ... and we tell him in our *own words*, what happened, right away ... well, then. *We* could calm him down. Calm him down and maybe he'll ... you know. Forgive us.

(Pause. MAX ponders this suggestion for a long moment. Then:)

MAX. Bobby. That is the stupidest idea I ever heard in my whole life.
BOBBY. You got gas in your car?
MAX. Yeah.
BOBBY. Then let's go.

(Blackout.)

Scene 3

(SETTING: MAX's car. Night. MAX drives. WE hear the sound of cars moving in the opposite direction—not too loud, so that it distracts, just gives a sense of atmosphere. Perhaps a suggestion of headlights flashing by from time to time.)

BOBBY. How far is Vermont, anyway?

MAX. I dunno. Six, seven hours—?

BOBBY. All night ride, eh? Like the old days when we used to drive out to south Jersey and pick up those casino payrolls? *(BOBBY laughs. A large truck passes, blowing its horn. The horn becomes a scream.)* Hey. Why are you stopping?

MAX. I—I'm not stopping. I'm turning around.

BOBBY. Turni—? *Why?*

MAX. Bobby ... *(MAX is about to say one thing—then reconsiders.)* ... I don't think this is such a terrific idea.

BOBBY. What? You got a *better* idea?

MAX. Yeah. Go home and hide.

BOBBY. *That's* a better idea?

MAX. I think so.

BOBBY. 'Member Tony Ramone? *He* tried to hide ...

MAX. What's with this, this "list" all of a sudden?

BOBBY. What "list?"

MAX. Of everybody who, you know, who, somethin' bad happened to 'em?

BOBBY. I'm just sayin'. You said "let's hide." I'm just remindin' you, Tony Ramone, *he* tried to hide! Yeah. Now he's underneath some parking lot in Jackson Heights someplace. *(Long pause. MAX sits, shaking his head.)* Look. Let's go talk to the Boss. He's human. He'll listen.

MAX. And what if he doesn't?

BOBBY. Just keep goin'. Okay? *(No answer.)* C'mon. Okay?

MAX. Bobby ... don't *do* this.

BOBBY. What? Do what?

MAX. You know.

BOBBY. No, I *don't* know. I just said, "What," didn't I? I don't know!

MAX. Don't cross me like this.

BOBBY. Cross you? I'm not crossin' you, Max, I'm just sayin'—

(MAX mimes pulling down a visor. Points to BOBBY's reflection in it.)

MAX. Look at you! Just look at yourself. That Italian suit ... imported cologne ... $75 haircut!

BOBBY. I know—

MAX. —You wouldn't have *any* a this if it wasn't for me!

BOBBY. I know.

MAX. *Huh?*

BOBBY. I *know*!

MAX. You'd still be collectin' garbage out in Floral Park—
BOBBY. Enough already.
MAX. Sweatin' like a pig in that V-neck T-shirt!
BOBBY. C'mon, okay?
MAX. Garbage man.
BOBBY. Shut up!
MAX. Garbage man!
BOBBY. *(Correcting him:)* Sanitation Worker.

(Beat; MAX just stares at BOBBY.)

MAX. *(The final word on the subject:) Garbage* man.

(Beat. BOBBY realizes he's lost this round.)

BOBBY. *(Almost like a pouting child:)* So?
MAX. So ... I *came back* for you!
BOBBY. I *know* that!
MAX. We grew up together, Bobby. That *means* somethin'! I came back for you and I *gave* you all this!
BOBBY. Max, I appreciate what you done for me. You know I do. I appreciate it!
MAX. Then how can you cross me like this?
BOBBY. I'm not crossin' you, okay? I just think we oughtta talk to the Boss! That's all! That's it! I just think that's the best thing to do!

(Long pause; MAX thinks about it. Then:)

MAX. Okay ...

(MAX pulls back onto the road.)

BOBBY. Just ... go and talk to him.
MAX. Yeah ...
BOBBY. You'll be glad.
MAX. Uh-huh.

(Beat.)

BOBBY. Are you okay?
MAX. Me?
BOBBY. I dunno. You seem all ...

MAX. I'm fine, Bobby. Don't worry about me. I'm fine.

(Pause. BOBBY makes an effort to lessen the tension:)

BOBBY. Hey. Maybe we can stop and get somethin' to eat soon. *(MAX looks at him.)* I'm gettin' kinda hungry.
    MAX. Hungry?
    BOOBY. Yeah.
    MAX. You had two platters of ziti.
    BOBBY. I know.
    MAX. And nine pieces of garlic bread.
    BOBBY Yeah?
    MAX. And two pieces of cheesecake!
    BOBBY. Is that *all*? No wonder I'm hungry!
    MAX. Good God ..
    BOBBY. I can't help it. I'm always extra hungry when we gotta kill somebody. It's my—you know, what do ya call it?
    MAX. Metabolism?
    BOBBY. Yeah, yeah. That's it. Metabolism. You know. *(Beat.)* So?
    MAX. What?
    BOBBY. Can we stop someplace? Denny's or IHOP, or, you know—
    MAX. Well—
    BOBBY. —someplace? I could really go for a stack a blueberry pancakes right about now! How 'bout you?
    MAX. I dunno ...
    BOBBY. C'mon!
    MAX. Well ... *(MAX checks his watch; beat.)* Maybe I *could* use a cup of coffee ... stretch my legs ...
    BOBBY. Okay then. IHOP it is!

(Blackout.)

Scene 4

(SETTING: International House of Pancakes. Muzak plays warped Lawrence Welk in the background. BOBBY and MAX sit at a table. BOBBY looks around.)

BOBBY. Where the hell's the waitress?

MAX. I dunno. Will you sit still?

BOBBY. I'm *hungry*! Look. They got All You Can Eat.

MAX. Yeah. Listen. We gotta figure out what we're gonna say.

BOBBY. I know what *I'm* gonna say: "Gimme a Big Stack of blueberry pancakes and a—"

MAX. —to the *Boss*!

BOBBY. Oh ...

MAX. Yeah.

(Beat.)

BOBBY. Listen. *You* figure it out, Max. You're a lot better with words than me. I don't wanna think about it right now ...

MAX. We *gotta* think about it, Bobby!

BOBBY. *(Waving MAX off with his hand:)* Ahh ... not 'till I got a full stomach. I can't think on a empty stomach.

MAX. Bobby. We gotta *talk* about this. We gotta get our stories straight!

BOBBY. Stories straight?

MAX. Yes.

BOBBY. S'nothin' to get straight. We just tell him what happened.

MAX. No, no, I don't think so.

(Beat.)

BOBBY. What, are you saying we oughtta *lie*?

MAX. Well ...

BOBBY. Are you saying we oughtta go up there and *lie* to the *Boss*?

MAX. I dunno. Maybe. Yeah.

BOBBY. Max, you can't lie to the Boss! That's like goin' into a confessional booth and lyin' to God!

MAX. The Boss ain't God, Bobby ...

BOBBY. Practically.

MAX. The Boss ain't God! *(Beat.)* Do you believe that God can, you know. Kill a guy?

MAX. I dunno.

BOBBY. Just—no, now, just answer the question. Do you believe that God can kill a guy? Like, say some guy sins or whatever, and God decides to take him out, do you think God could kill the guy?

MAX. I dunno ... I guess so, yeah.

BOBBY. Okay. Good. Now ... do you think the Boss can kill a guy?

MAX. Yeah.

BOBBY. So, then, there ya go.

MAX. Bobby ...

BOBBY. Look I *know* the Boss could kill me. Like *that*—*(BOBBY snaps his fingers.)* I am *not* gonna mess around with the Boss!

MAX. But Bobby ... hey, look. I got an idea, see.

BOBBY. What?

MAX. Lemme show you.

BOBBY. Show me?

MAX. Okay. Look. *(He moves the salt and pepper shakers around on the table.)* Let's say that this table top is Grand Central Station—

BOBBY. *(Shouting off:)* Could we get some *service* here?

MAX. Watch, willya? I'm tryin' to show you somethin'.

BOBBY. Well, she's just standin' there, smokin' a cigarette. Look at her! *(BOBBY calls out, very loudly:)* Hey, you! Yeah! You! What the hell do we gotta do to get waited on in this joint? *(Apparently the unseen waitress hears this and flips him the bird. He returns the gesture.)* Yeah? You too! *(BOBBY turns to MAX:)* Can you *believe* that? People's manners have gone right down the toilet ...

MAX. Just watch, okay. I'm trying to show you something here—

BOBBY. Okay, okay. I'm watchin'.

(BOBBY takes out nail clippers, prepares to trim his nails.)

MAX. *(Demonstrating with the salt and pepper shakers:)* All right. The table top is Grand Central. Okay? And the salt and pepper shakers are you and me.

BOBBY. Wait a minute, whoa, now. Hold up.

MAX. What?

BOBBY. Who's the black one?

(Beat.)

MAX. What?

BOBBY. I don't wanna be the black one!

MAX. Bobby. I'm being serious here—

BOBBY. I know. So am I. I don't wanna be the *black* one!

MAX. Bobby—

BOBBY. *(In overexaggerated "black" dialect:)* Yeah, yeah, okay, baby! Show me de Gran' Central Station thang.

MAX. Shut *up*, will you? I got an idea, see.

BOBBY. Le's see yo' idea, boy!

MAX. I'm warning you.

BOBBY. *(Himself again:)* Okay, okay. So show me.

(BOBBY, watching, begins clipping his nails.)

MAX. Okay. Now. So we're here. That's you and that's me. And this thing—*(One of those paper "specials" standees.)*—is the stairs from Metro North. And this—*(MAX reacts to BOBBY's nail clipping:)* Will you cut that out? You got me in the eye with one of your fingernails!

BOBBY. I'm sorry. I'll aim lower.

MAX. What the hell are you doing?

BOBBY. I wanna be well-groomed when we see the Boss.

MAX. *(Grabbing the clippers:)* Will you pay attention!

BOBBY. Hey! Don't lose those!

MAX. I won't. Okay? Now watch.

BOBBY. I'm always losin' those.

MAX. PAY ATTENTION! *(Beat.)* Okay. Now. We're standing by the phones, right? And we see this guy coming up the stairs towards the phones—

BOBBY. *(Looking around:)* Now look. She's gone. Where the hell is she now? On the toilet?

MAX. WATCH! *(BOBBY does.)* This—*(He gestures to the cream container.)*—is the guy we did—the *wrong* guy. Okay. So he comes towards the phones ... right?

BOBBY. Yeah ...

MAX. ... and we see him. And, presumably, the *right* guy—*(MAX moves a syrup container into the "scene.")* —gets off the train and we don't see *him* 'cause we're busy sticking the wrong guy. *(BOBBY takes out lots of sugar and Sweet n' Low packets and strews them all over the table top.)* Wha—what are you doing?

BOBBY. I'm makin' it realismic.

MAX. What the hell is that?

BOBBY. S'all the *bums* in Grand Central. Hey. Can I have my clippers back now? *(MAX flings the clippers offstage.)* Hey!

MAX. *(Knocking the stuff off the table top:)* Forget it! Okay? I'm not gonna show you! I had a really good idea and you—ah, the hell with it. The hell with you!

(MAX rises.)

BOBBY. What are you doin'?

MAX. I'm leaving! I'm going back to Long Island—

BOBBY. Max, c'mon—

MAX. You're not taking this seriously, so why the hell should I take it seriously—?

BOBBY. I am! I am, I'm takin' it real seriously, but c'mon, you gotta admit, salt and pepper shakers?

MAX. You are such a pain in the ass ...

(MAX starts to walk out.)

BOBBY. (Calling after him.) Max—! *(MAX goes. Pause. BOBBY looks around for the waitress, starts to pick up some of the sugar packets. He pockets a few. He looks up at an imaginary customer who is apparently staring at him. To the imaginary customer:)* What are you lookin' at?

(BOBBY sits down and starts to look at the menu, looks around for the waitress again. After a few moments, MAX re-enters.)

MAX. If you're coming, come on.

BOBBY. *(Torn between the menu and MAX:)* Where we going?

(They stare at each other. Blackout.)

Scene 5

(SETTING: The car. Later. Both are tired. BOBBY drives. MAX writes on his legal pad. After a long moment of silence, BOBBY looks over. MAX is absorbed and doesn't notice. BOBBY is bored. He looks at MAX again, then reaches for the radio.)

MAX. *(Without looking up:)* Don't turn that on.

BOBBY. I can't help it. I'm bored. I'm fallin' asleep.

MAX. Roll down the window.

BOBBY. That don't help, it just stinks out there.

MAX. It's called *countryside*.

BOBBY. I don't care what it's called; it *stinks*!

MAX. Are you kidding? New-mown grass ... hay ...

BOBBY. *(Holding his nose:)* It makes me want to puke.

MAX. You probably think the City smells *good*.

BOBBY. The City don't smell at *all*.

MAX. What?

BOBBY. The City don't smell!

MAX. Are you kidding me? Of *course* it smells!

BOBBY. No it don't. It's—whatcha call it—neutered.

MAX. It stinks! Like vomit and piss ...

BOBBY. Not once you get used to it. Once you get used to it, it don't smell at all. You know. Immuned.

MAX. *You're* used to it?

BOBBY. Sure.

MAX. You're sick.

(BEAT. MAX returns to his pad.)

BOBBY. What the hell is it you're writing anyway?

MAX. Nothing.

BOBBY. You been goin' like gangbusters on that for weeks now. What is it?

MAX. Nothing.

BOBBY. Lemme see—

MAX. Bobby—

BOBBY. Lemme see it!

MAX. No!

BOBBY. Give it here!

(BOBBY reaches for it. They swerve; a car horn blares. BOBBY regains control of the car.)

MAX. WILL YOU WATCH THE ROAD? LOOK OUT! *(Silence. BOBBY keeps hoping MAX will talk about his writing. MAX senses this. Finally:)* It's *ideas*, Bobby.

BOBBY. Ideas—?

MAX. Something you obviously don't have.

(Beat.)

BOBBY. Hah. Don't *have*. I don't—? Hah! I got *lotsa* ideas. *Lots.* "I don't have ideas ... "

MAX. Tell me one.

BOBBY. What?

MAX. Tell me one idea you've got.

BOBBY. You mean—?

MAX. Just tell me.

BOBBY. You mean, just *say* it?

MAX. Yeah.
BOBBY. Say it out loud?
MAX. Yeah.
BOBBY. Just tell you what it is.
MAX. One idea. Tell me one idea that's in your head.

(Beat. BOBBY thinks.)

BOBBY. I gotta take a leak. *(Beat.)* How's that?
MAX. That's *it*?
BOBBY. Yeah.
MAX. Bobby ...
BOBBY. What?
MAX. You call that an *idea*?
BOBBY. (Insulted:) Whasamatter with *that*?
MAX. Never mind ...
BOBBY. Whasamatter with it?
MAX. It's—*(Too hard to explain:)* Nothing.
BOBBY. It's what? It's what? What is it?
MAX. Never mind.
BOBBY. It's *stupid*.
MAX. No ...
BOBBY. That's what you were gonna say, ain't it? "It's stupid."
MAX. No.
BOBBY. You still think a me like a stupid garbage man.
MAX. No I don't.
BOBBY. You *do*!
MAX. Enough!

(Beat.)

BOBBY. Okay, then. Let's hear one a *yours*.
MAX. One a my what?
BOBBY. Ideas!
MAX. Bobby ...
BOBBY. Well, If mine's so ... *insulting* to you; let's hear one a your big ideas that you been writing in there.
MAX. One a my ideas?
BOBBY. Yeah.
MAX. You want me to *tell* you one of my ideas.
BOBBY. Yeah.

(Beat.)

MAX. We are criminals, Bobby. You and me. We kill, we take advantage of the weak, we live like parasites off the rest of society. Are we *born* into this? Or do we grow into it? Do we seek it? Do we crave it? Or are we pre-destined to live it to the end? How does Original Sin fit into *our* world? How does it relate to the wrongs we belch forth into the World? Modern society is crumbling all around us and how responsible are *we* for that? How heavy do our sins weigh in the scale of civilization? Is there a way for redemption? For escape? What is our path of escape?

(Long pause.)

BOBBY. And that's better'n *mine*? *(MAX's head drops in frustration.)* At least mine made *sense*! "I gotta take a leak." A guy could hear that and know what it *means*. But you, I don't have the slightest idea what the hell you're talking about, "how heavy do our sins weigh in the scale of civilization?" What is that, huh? What the hell is *that*? *(Long pause.)* There's a rest stop. I'm gonna pull over and take a leak.

(Blackout.)

Scene 6

(SETTING: Rest area. MAX and BOBBY face upstage, as if urinating in a trough urinal, side-by-side.)

BOBBY. I'm sorry, Max. I didn't mean to rag on you about your writing. I figgered you's sittin' over there makin' up what we were gonna say to the Boss. I just wanted to know.

(MAX zips up his pants and turns to face us, walks down center and mimes checking himself out in a mirror. He takes out a pocket comb and combs his hair.)

MAX. You wouldn't listen to my *last* idea about what to tell the Boss.
BOBBY. *(Black voice:)* You mean wid de salt an' peppah shakers?
MAX. Fuck you.

BOBBY. Can I borrow your comb?

MAX. Here. *(BOBBY uses it, offers it back.)* Keep it. You got dandruff.

BOBBY. Oh—*(BOBBY looks in the "mirror" and is very, very upset:)* —NO! And we're gonna be seein' the Boss!

(BOBBY busies himself, brushing off his shoulders.)

MAX. My whole idea back at the IHOP was—

BOBBY. *(Of his appearance:)* How's that?

MAX. Good—was, that we tell him we never *saw* the guy.

(Beat.)

BOBBY. What guy? The guy we did?

MAX. *Any* guy. *(Pause. BOBBY thinks about this.)* How's he gonna know we did *any*body? *(BOBBY starts to answer.)* —He's not *gonna* know. Unless we tell him.

BOBBY. *(The light bulb goes on:)* Oh ... so, we just say, we never saw *nobody* that fit the, ah, the—

MAX. Yeah.

BOBBY. —the description.

MAX. Yeah!

(Beat.)

BOBBY. So, then ... he *can't* be mad.

MAX. Right.

BOBBY. Cause we didn't do nothin' wrong.

MAX. Uh-huh ...

BOBBY. Cause, as far as we know, the *guy* ...

MAX. ... yeah ... ?

BOBBY. ... wasn't even on the *train*!

MAX. Exactly!

(They laugh. A moment of camaraderie. Then we hear a toilet flush. They look in the direction of the stall. Did somebody hear them? Blackout.)

Scene 7

(SETTING: In the blackout, we hear a scream. As the lights come up on MAX's car again, the scream turns into the sound of a car horn as a car swerves, passing in the opposite direction. MAX is driving. BOBBY is asleep. MAX veers to avoid the swerving car. The sudden motion wakes BOBBY.)

BOBBY. Huh—? Wha—?
MAX. *(Introspective and very troubled:)* We crossed the line, Bobby.

(BOBBY blinks, tries to wake.)

BOBBY. What?
MAX. *(Covering his thoughts:)* The, ah, the Vermont State Line.
BOBBY. Hey. Wow. We're in Vermont already?
MAX. Yeah.
BOBBY. *(Yawning:)* What time is it?
MAX. Around three.
BOBBY. Jeez. We made good time.
MAX. I been going 80.

(Pause.)

BOBBY. Could we stop someplace and *sleep*? You know. How far's the Boss's place?
MAX. Another hour.
BOBBY. Aw, let's *stop* someplace.
MAX. You think?
BOBBY. Why not? Either that, or we're gonna hafta sleep in the car.
MAX. Yeah, but if I fall into a bed, I'll *never* wake up.
BOBBY. You'll wake up. I'll get you up. Don't worry. I'll get you up. Although you are a pretty sound sleeper ... hmm. *(BOBBY remembers something, begins to laugh.)* You remember that time in Philly? We stayed out all night, and you met that girl? Took her up to your room, and you just kinda ... passed out! Remember? She couldn't wake you up, she thought you was dead! *(MAX begins to laugh along with BOBBY.)* She called the cops. Remember? She thought she had given you a—a heart attack! And when you finally wake up—you remember this? You finally wake up—

MAX. —there's all these *cops* standing over me!

BOBBY. You though they were arrestin' you!

MAX. I know, I know! I thought, this is how it ends. I get caught layin' in bed butt naked! And then *you* came in—

BOBBY. —and told 'em I was your *lawyer*!

(They're BOTH really laughing now. This goes on for a bit, then laughter subsides.)

MAX. Yeah, you saved my ass, Bobby. You literally saved my bare ass!

BOBBY. Hey. What would you expect, huh? You'd a done the same for me.

MAX. Yeah ...

(Silence for a moment.)

BOBBY. C'mon. Let's stop. I won't let you oversleep. *(No answer.)* C'mon ... *(Pause.)* Look. There's a Days Inn.

MAX. I *hate* Days Inn.

(Beat; they drive on for a bit in silence.)

BOBBY. There's a Motel 6.

MAX. I like Motel 6.

BOBBY. Okay then.

(MAX turns. Blackout.)

Scene 8

(SETTING: Motel room. MAX tries to get settled for bed. BOBBY paces and fidgets.)

MAX. I thought you wanted to sleep.

BOBBY. I know. But now I'm awake.

MAX. Good God!

BOBBY. I can't help it! *(Beat.)* Maybe I oughtta go out and grab a fifth. That'd be fun, wouldn't it? If we had us a fifth?

MAX. Yeah, like I *really* wanna show up at the Boss's house reeking of booze with dandruff all over my jacket. *(BOBBY takes this as a hint and brushes off his shoulder.)* C'mon. Do us *both* a favor and just get some sleep. We're both gonna be jumpy when we see him.

BOBBY. You go on. I'm gonna sit up for awhile.
MAX. Okay.

(MAX turns over in the bed and prepares to sleep. A pause. BOBBY notices the television.)

BOBBY. Can I cut on the TV?
MAX. No.
BOBBY. They got cable.
MAX. No.

(Pause. BOBBY looks around the room.)

BOBBY. Maybe they got Room Service.
MAX. What?
BOBBY. You want me to call down to the desk, see if they got—
MAX. What the hell do you think this place is, the Ritz Carlton? They don't have room service!
BOBBY. Well, maybe they got some vending machines. Something. I could go for a Mars Bar right about now.
MAX. You're hungry *again*?
BOBBY. I can't help it. It's my, you know—
MAX. —metabolism.
BOBBY. Yeah. You know.
MAX. Look. Go get yourself a Mars bar and let me go to sleep, all right?

(BOBBY starts for the door, fishing in his pocket for change. He looks at what he has, stops.)

BOBBY. Max? *(MAX pulls his pillow over his head.)* You got any change?
MAX. *(From under his pillow.)* No!
BOBBY. All I need's a quarter.
MAX. Bobby, shuttup. All right? I'm not gonna tell you again. Shuttup and let me go to sleep. I mean it! *(Pause. BOBBY starts to look around the room, moving close to MAX's bed. He stops and peers over at MAX. MAX's eyes pop open.)* WHAT?
BOBBY. Where's your newspaper? *(No answer.)* Max? *(No answer.)* Look, just tell me where your newspaper is and I'll leave you alone.

MAX. *(Barely awake:)* On the table.

(BOBBY gets the newspaper, sits down and starts to look at it. Glances up and sees MAX's notepad nearby. Beat. He looks at it. Looks at MAX. He sure would like to sneak a peak at it, but—no, he'd better not. He opens the paper again, tries to concentrate. He can't. Boy, he'd really like to get ahold of that legal pad! Is it safe? He looks at MAX. Why not? He reaches for the legal pad and starts to read. Lights slowly fade on BOBBY but a spotlight remains on MAX, who has begun to toss fitfully in his sleep. Sounds of screaming and of someone pleading, begging for his life begin to rise in volume as MAX tosses and turns in the bed. Lights fade so that we're left in blackness with sounds of violence and mayhem. Blackout.)

Scene 9

(SETTING: The hotel room. In the black, we hear the screaming from the end of Scene 8. A spotlight comes up on MAX's face as he sleeps. MAX squirms in his sleep. Then another scream, a little louder this time. MAX thrashes in bed as we hear another and then another scream on top of that one, more and more, all running together to finally form one big aural tapestry of fear and screams. MAX leaps up in his bed from the nightmare. Lights return to normal. It is silent. BOBBY sits in his chair holding a fifth. He stares at MAX. He is drunk. Light streams in.)

MAX. Sorry. I had a—
BOBBY. What?
MAX. —a dream. I had a dream.
BOBBY. Nightmare, eh?

(MAX picks up his watch from the bedside table. His eyes bug out.)

MAX. Bobby!
BOBBY. Did you have a nightmare, Max?
MAX. Oh my God ...
BOBBY. Did you have a nightmare?
MAX. It's ten o'clock!
BOBBY. It is? Huh. I kinda lost track around dawn ...

(BOBBY drinks from his fifth.)

MAX. Bobby!
BOBBY. What?
MAX. Are you drinking?
BOBBY. Me?
MAX. Bobby—!
BOBBY. Yes, Max. I am drinking. As a matter of fact, I'm *drunk!*
(BOBBY laughs, offers MAX the bottle:) Want one?
MAX. I *told* you not to go get a bottle! Didn't I specifically say not to go buy a bottle?
BOBBY. I didn't *buy* this, Max. No. You thought I *bought* this? Hah! I wished for it, Max. Yeah, I sat here and wished for it and it fell from heaven. Right into my lap. See? I got ideas too. Maybe I oughtta try writin' a *book!*

(Silence. That last remark was pointed, and MAX hesitates.)

MAX. Book—?
BOBBY. I read your book, Max.
MAX. Bobby—
BOBBY. I BET YOU DIDN'T THINK I COULD *READ!* But I read your book—

(BOBBY waves the legal pad.)

MAX. You son of a bitch! That's personal!
BOBBY. Personal? It's all about you and me, Max! Yeah, damn right it's personal! It's mine *too!*

(Beat.)

MAX. Look. I don't know what you're thinking. But, it—it's not a book. It—it's like a diary, see? Just my *ideas*—
BOBBY. Ideas, huh?
MAX. Yes.
BOBBY. Pretty profitable ideas, eh? Well, I guess this *letter*'s just an "idea" too, eh Max?

(BOBBY holds up a letter.)

MAX. Give that to me—
BOBBY. *(Reading the letter:)* "Per our conversation, enclosed

please find a check for $50,000 as an advance against future royalties. We were quite impressed with chapters 1 - 10 of your novel BLOOD ON OUR HANDS and we look forward—"

MAX. *(Out of bed now, grabbing the letter:)* You son of a bitch! That was NONE of your business!

BOBBY. Whose is it then?

MAX. You shouldn't a read that.

BOBBY. Max! It's all about *us*! You told about all the people we killed ... the guy in Boston, that fella in the East Village with the hubcaps ... you got stories about the Boss in here and Little Joey Carmello in here—

(MAX has begun hastily dressing.)

MAX. So?
BOBBY. *So*? You can't *tell* about all that! You can't *do* that!
MAX. Bobby. I changed all the names.

(MAX puts on his holster, picks his gun up from the night stand and checks to see if it is still loaded.)

BOBBY. So? You still *told*! Jeez, Max. You got any idea what the Boss is gonna do when he finds out?

(On hearing this, MAX freezes where he stands, still holding the gun.)

MAX. The Boss is *not* gonna find out, Bobby. *(Pause. BOBBY says nothing. MAX turns and slowly walks over to BOBBY, still holding the gun.)* The Boss is not gonna find out.

(BOBBY looks at MAX. Their eyes hold. Tableau of BOBBY sitting there looking up at MAX and MAX holding the gun. Act I must end with us asking the question, "is MAX going to use it?" Blackout.)

END OF ACT I

ACT II

Scene 1

(SETTING: A diner counter. At rise, MAX is alone at the counter, stirring a cup of coffee. After the scene is established, BOBBY enters as if from the restroom. As BOBBY sinks onto the stool next to MAX [visibly hungover], MAX slides the coffee over to BOBBY.)

MAX. Drink it.
BOBBY. I don't want it.
MAX. You want something to eat?
BOBBY. No. *(Beat.)* Maybe. I dunno ... Like what?
MAX. I dunno ... *(MAX consults the menu.)* Hey, they got blueberry pancakes—
BOBBY. *(Gagging.)* Don't make me sick ...
MAX. You wanted 'em last night!
BOBBY. That was last night!

(Beat.)

MAX. Here. Drink this.
BOBBY. No.
MAX. Drink it. *(Beat.)* You'd better drink it. We gotta sober you up.
BOBBY. Get outta my face ...
MAX. Do you want me to dump it down your throat? C'MON! DRINK!

(Beat; BOBBY obeys. MAX looks around. BOBBY grimaces at the taste of the coffee, adds lots and lots of sugar under the following:)

BOBBY. You wanna know what pisses me off the most?
MAX. What?
BOBBY. That I got the hands of a woman!

33

MAX. What?

BOBBY. That's what you said! In your book, you said "he had the hands of a woman."

MAX. I did not.

BOBBY. You did! A *woman*!

MAX. I didn't mean it *that* way.

BOBBY. Hah.

MAX. It was nothing. It was just—you know.

BOBBY. What?

MAX. You know. *(Beat.)* Never mind.

BOBBY. What? It was what? They're *my* hands, I wanna know! These hands have killed people! They collected garbage for five years! They've felt up some a the hottest girls on Long Island! And *you* got the balls to call 'em the hands of a *woman*? All these people out there, Max, all these people are gonna read your book and they're gonna think I'm some kinda faggot!

MAX. I was just being ... you know. Literary.

BOBBY. Literary?

MAX. That's right.

BOBBY. Fuck. You. Ernest Hemingway.

MAX. Look, I'll *change* it, all right?

BOBBY. I don't care what you do ...

MAX. Anyway, I didn't say that you had the hands of a woman.

BOBBY. Yes you did!

MAX. I *did* not! What I *said* was, your hands were "almost feminine in the grace they expressed when driving the knife home." Here. See?

(MAX fumbles through the manuscript to find the spot. BOBBY waves him off.)

BOBBY. I read it already.

MAX. I just wanna show you—

BOBBY. I don't wanna lookit that!

MAX. —it's a compliment! It's saying you're graceful in what you do! It's Poetic!

BOBBY. Hah.

MAX. Okay. Watch me. I'm changin' it. *(MAX starts to change it with a pen. Stops.)* But I *meant* it as a compliment.

BOBBY. Well, thanks a lot.

(Pause. BOBBY nurses his coffee. MAX looks around. Then:)

MAX. Bobby. Listen to me. You're not gonna ... say anything, are you? *(BOBBY looks at MAX quizzically.)* To the Boss. *(No answer.)* Bobby. You can't say anything.

BOBBY. Yeah, and why not?

MAX. Cause. You know.

BOBBY. Yeah, I know. I'm not supposed to talk. But *you* talked plenty! You got $50,000 for saying I look like a woman—

MAX. Bobby—

BOBBY. —and the *Boss*, Max! *(Realizes he's loud, BOBBY brings it down:)* Max, you said the Boss resembled a spoiled, angry bulldog with rotted teeth!

MAX. *(Correcting him:)* "Abscessed teeth."

BOBBY. What's the difference?

MAX. I'm not talking about his dental hygiene! I was trying to convey that he was irritable.

BOBBY. Max!

MAX. Well, he *is*!

BOBBY. Max, how can you sit there? How can you sit there and tell me not to say anything when you've already said it *all*?

MAX. Bobby ... listen.

BOBBY. I'm listening!

MAX. I'm gonna lay something on you, okay?

BOBBY. Yeah ...

MAX. It's gonna sound pretty weird.

BOBBY. Weirder than me bein' told I look like a faggot?

MAX. Bobby, please.

BOBBY. What?

(Beat.)

MAX. I hear voices.

(Beat. BOBBY looks around.)

BOBBY. Well ... of course you hear voices, there's a coupla dozen people in this place, Max—

MAX. No, no, in my head. In my *dreams* at night.

(Pause. BOBBY is taken aback.)

BOBBY. *(Warily:)* Max ... Don't be messin' with me, okay?

MAX. I'm not.

BOBBY. Don't mess with me.

MAX. I'm not! I'm telling you the *truth*!

(Beat.)

BOBBY. What do you mean, voices? Like, people talking to you and stuff?

MAX. Not exactly.

BOBBY. Cause my Aunt Carlotta, she heard stuff like that. She was always hearin' Abraham Lincoln readin' the Declaration of Independence to her or some kind a bullshit. So they gave her shock treatment and form then on, the only thing she could hear was a fuckin' dog whistle!

MAX. No, no, Bobby, it's not like that. It—look. I want you to understand.

(Beat. MAX take a deep breath, then:)

MAX. I wanna quit.
BOBBY. Quit?
MAX. Yeah.
BOBBY. Quit what?
MAX. *This*!
BOBBY. What, workin' for the Boss?
MAX. Takin' advantage of people! Killin' people! BEIN' A CRIMINAL. I wanna start over ...
BOBBY. What, by writin' this *book*?
MAX. I dunno. Yeah. I'm thinkin' maybe take that money and use it to start over. I'm gonna get some regular *job* someplace and see what happens.
BOBBY. What happens? I'll *tell* you what'll happen: the Boss'll come after you and slice your NUTS off, is what'll happen!
MAX. He doesn't *have* to know. *(Beat.)* The Boss *doesn't have to know* about this book! *(Pause.)* Bobby, I want to have a home. I wanna fall in love, I wanna have a wife, and kids, and come home from work at night and eat dinner with 'em and I wanna worry about how to fix a hot water heater and whether we have enough money to roof the house. I *want* that. I *don't* wanna be slipping around in train stations for the rest a my life, stabbing guys in pay toilets.
BOBBY. *I* was the one who stabbed him.
MAX. Bobby. I wanna get out.

(Beat.)

BOBBY. Are you gonna tell the Boss?

Beat.)

MAX. I dunno ...

BOBBY. Were you gonna tell *me*?

MAX. Yes. I was. Look. Bobby. I can't take this anymore.

BOBBY. What?

MAX. *This!* All this—you don't know ... Every night, I wake up, hearing these voices! Every night I can't sleep! It doesn't matter if the lights are on or if I'm by myself or I'm with somebody, it doesn't matter cause I still hear the screaming, Bobby! The screaming voices of all the people we've killed!

BOBBY. *You* didn't kill them, Max. *I* killed 'em.

MAX. I HELPED YOU! I'm part of it! I've got blood on *my* hands too!

BOBBY. You wash your hands, Max. The blood comes off.

MAX. Don't you ever *hear* them? Crying out to you? *(BOBBY shakes his head "no.")* I do. Screaming, calling out to me, demanding my soul!

BOBBY. Max, aren't you gettin' a little over-dramatic here?

MAX. You read my book, Bobby! You *know* how it haunts me! It eats away at me! What we do, we're gonna have to pay for it! We can't just keep doing it a doing it and *never* pay for it! That's why I gotta get away. Go. Then maybe the voices will stop. I don't know how else to stop them, Bobby. I don't know. But you gotta see, that's what's behind this book. I'm not doin' it to make money. I'm not doin' it to be some big shot or anything like that. I'm doing it for survival. This is what I got to do to survive. So you can't say nothing to the Boss, you understand?

Pause.)

BOBBY. You are *really* screwed-up, you know that?

MAX. Bobby. You can't. Say. Anything.

BOBBY. Why would I talk? I mean, you know. I've *never* talked. To nobody. This stuff between us, it stays with us. That's just how it is. You know that.

MAX. I know. I know, I just don't want you to—you know.

BOBBY. What?

MAX. Nothing.

BOBBY. No, you don't want me to—"what?" What?

MAX. Try to make this into a Merit Badge.

(Pause.)

BOBBY. You shit.
MAX. Bobby—
BOBBY. You piece of—
MAX. Shhh!
BOBBY. All these years!
MAX. Bobby, keep it down!
BOBBY. All these years, you sorry son of a bitch! And now. *This*
MAX. Hey, hey—
BOBBY. This is all the trust I get? Never once in all these year
did I ever talk! *Never!*
MAX. Bobby! People are looking at us—
BOBBY. *(Casting a dangerous look at the unseen others aroun*
them:) LET 'EM LOOK!

(BEAT.)

MAX. I'm sorry, Bobby.
BOBBY. Yeah. You're "sorry." *(BOBBY looks at another imagi*
nary customer.) What're *you* lookin' at? *(Then, to MAX:)* Pay the
tab. Let's go.
MAX. Bobby, maybe we should wait—
BOBBY. Wait? Until what? Huh? I sober up? I'm *sober*, okay
We've waited long enough. Let's go.

(BOBBY starts walking off. Blackout.)

Scene 2

(SETTING: The BOSS's yard. White iron lawn furniture.)

BOSS. Boys!
BOBBY. Boss!
MAX. Hi Boss ...
BOSS. It's good to see you two up in the country.
MAX. Well, it—it's good to *be* here ...
BOBBY. Yeah. It *smells* good up here!

(Beat.)

BOSS. You boys want anything? A drink, maybe?

MAX. *(Worried about BOBBY:)* Ah ...

BOBBY. Well, maybe for Max, here. Not for me, though. Too early in the day for *me* ...

BOSS. Aha! Discipline! I like to see that in one a my boys ... Here, have a seat. *(They do.)* Ah, I tell ya. You boys are like sons to me, did I ever tell you that? Real sons. I don't spend enough time with you, talking to you, showing you the ropes ... I gotta get into the City more, be more of a Father to my boys, eh? *(The BOSS laughs.)* Say. Do you know what today is?

BOBBY. Today?

MAX. Ah ...

BOSS. Today is the *first day* of spring!

BOBBY. First day of spring, eh?

MAX. I didn't realize that ...

BOBBY. Must be why it *smells* so good, huh?

BOSS. Oh, the woods are *alive*, boys! They're breaking forth with new life for the year ahead! *(The BOSS suddenly explodes, violently:)* GODDAMMIT!

BOBBY. What is it?

BOSS. Look!

BOBBY. What?

BOSS. There!

MAX. Where?

BOSS. I can't *believe* it!

MAX. What?

BOSS. *(Pointing to a piece of the lawn furniture:)* That fucking CHAIR!

(Beat.)

BOBBY. What ... about it?

BOSS. *(Getting dangerously angry now:)* That little BASTARD!

MAX. Who?

BOSS. I'm gonna kill him! I swear to God, I am gonna rip his balls off one at a time and nail 'em to a fuckin' tree!

(The BOSS whips out a gun.)

MAX. Ooh, Boss!

BOBBY. Boss, take it easy!

BOSS. *(Calling off:)* Peppino? Peppino, come here! Boss's got something for you! *(Back to BOBBY and MAX:)* I'm sure he's hiding.

They're always hiding, when you want them. That makes me so goddamn MAD!

MAX. Boss, take it easy—

BOSS. Don't tell me to take it easy! That little Mexican Houseboy BASTARD! You try to be nice, y'know, but they just take ADVANTAGE! HOW MANY FUCKING TIMES DO I HAVE TO *TELL* HIM? THE CHAIR *GOES HERE*! *(The BOSS moves the chair about an inch. Not much at all. He takes a few moments to catch his breath. He calms.)* So ... what can I do for my two boys? I hope nothing's *wrong*.

BOBBY. Oh, no, no, no—

MAX. Not at all ...

BOSS. Uh-huh. *(Beat. The BOSS seems to have regained composure. He returns the gun to its shoulder holster.)* You fellas had an appointment last night, am I right?

(Beat; they look at each other.)

BOBBY. Yeah. Well ...
MAX. Yeah, we did, Boss.
BOSS. Uh-huh ...
BOBBY. But ... he didn't show, Boss.

(Beat.)

BOSS. Didn't show?
BOBBY. Nah.
MAX. We wanted to come out here and tell you.
BOBBY. In person.

(Beat.)

BOSS. You mean, you boys came all the way out here just to tell me some guy didn't *show*?
MAX. Well—
BOBBY. Yeah.

(Beat.)

BOSS. Look! Did you see that?
MAX. *(Reaching for his gun.)* What?
BOSS. A fox!
MAX. Huh?

BOBBY. A fox?

BOSS. Baby fox. Look at that coat!

MAX. *(Relaxing now:)* Imagine that ...

BOSS. Yeah. It's rare, you see a little fox like that, running around out here near people's houses.

MAX. Ah ...

BOSS. Baby fox is very vulnerable when it's away from its mother and father.

BOBBY. Uh-huh ...

BOSS. A baby fox is liable to get killed by some other carnivore if it strays too far from home.

BOBBY. Huh.

BOSS. *(This is funny to him:)* —unless of course some hunter has blown its mother's head off, then it don't have no choice!

(The BOSS laughs.)

MAX. Ha-ha.

BOBBY. Yeah, that's true ...

(The BOSS goes into a coughing fit. It lasts for a long, long time. It sounds like he's about to cough his lungs up. It finally subsides.)

MAX. Can we get you anything, Boss?

BOSS. Yeah. Gimme a cigarette. *(BOBBY does. Both BOBBY and MAX frantically produce cigarette lighters. The BOSS studies both of them, then allows MAX to light it. Beat. BOBBY seems wounded by this gesture.)* That's how I was when I started out in this business, boys. A baby fox. All by myself, lost in the woods. When I came to New York in 1947 at the age of 14, I didn't have a parent to watch after me, either. I hadda learn all the ins and outs by myself.

MAX. You've done real well for yourself, Boss.

BOBBY. Yeah. You told us one time that you got your start picking pockets on Madison Avenue.

BOSS. That's right! Fourteen years old and I was taking home more money than most a the fellas I was robbing! Boy, *those* were the days ... and then, I met the man who was, to me, what I am to you. The Boss. And he *made* me. I can never pay him back for what he did for me. Gave me my start in life. Was a father to me. You know what it says in the Bible, doncha?

MAX. Ah ...

BOBBY. Gee, ah ...

BOSS. "Honor thy father and mother." Do you know what that means?

MAX. Ah ...

BOSS. That means you don't screw around with your father, eh?

MAX and BOBBY. Oh, yeah. You're right. Uh-huh, etc.

BOSS. Ah, look at you boys. You're really a sight, you know that? Not like the old days. You boys got a lot on the ball. College educated. You're college-educated, aren't you?

BOBBY. I'm not, Boss. Max is.

MAX. Well ... Junior College. Two years.

BOSS. Junior college! Imagine that! Back when I was comin' up through the ranks, we never even dreamed about gettin' an education. Didn't have time for it. But you boys ... and lookit them suits! Turn around. *(They do.)* You look like successful men. Not like a coupla greaseballs from Carmine Street. Yessir, things have changed all right. Things have really changed. You boys are a New Breed. A Whole New Breed. *(Beat.)* So. What's the problem, eh? You tell me you didn't do the guy last night, s'that it?

MAX. That's right, Boss.

BOSS. He wasn't there.

MAX. No.

BOSS. He didn't show.

BOBBY. No.

BOSS. Well, now ... I happen to know for a fact that he *did* show.

(Pause.)

BOBBY. Ah ...

BOSS. It seems another of your brothers saw him last night. *Late* last night. I asked if he was leaking blood, I said, "I know he's got a hole the size of Nebraska in him, my *boys* took care of him." But they assured me he was fine. He was in perfect health.

BOBBY. Well, Boss, y'see—

MAX. We had a little mishap.

BOSS. Mishap, huh?

BOBBY. Yeah.

MAX. Y'see—

BOBBY. Ah ...

MAX. Bobby stabbed the wrong guy.

(Silence. BOBBY looks at MAX. If looks could kill, this would suddenly be a two-character scene.)

BOSS. Is this true, Bobby? *(No answer.)* Bobby?

BOBBY. *(Barely audible:)* Yeah, ah—it's true ...

BOSS. You stabbed the wrong guy?

BOBBY. *(Not said, perhaps, just nodded:)* Yeah ...

MAX. *(An attempt to stem the damage he's done:)* This guy, though, Boss, this guy, he was exactly like the description you gave me, so—

(The BOSS raises a hand to silence MAX.)

BOSS. *(To BOBBY:)* You stabbed the wrong guy.

BOBBY. Yeah, Boss. I did.

(Long pause.)

BOSS. Some animals eat their young. Did you boys know that? I don't know about foxes ... but some wild animals, they devour their young. *(Silence for a moment. Then:)* Max. Maybe you'd better go on back to the Island.

MAX. Yeah, but Boss—

BOSS. Maybe you'd better head back to the Island.

(Long pause.)

MAX. Alone?

(Pause. BOSS does not look at MAX; he's been staring at BOBBY, who in turn is focused on his feet.)

BOSS. Alone.

(Pause. MAX goes. BOBBY and the BOSS sit in silence for a few moments. Then:)

BOSS. Max.

BOBBY. I'm Bobby.

BOSS. I know. I said "Max."

BOBBY. Oh. *(Beat.)* How come?

BOSS. Cause. I'm thinking about him.

BOBBY. Oh.

BOSS. He seems a little ...

(Pause.)

BOBBY. A little what?

BOSS. Jumpy.

BOBBY. Oh.

BOSS. I wonder why that is.

BOBBY. I dunno.

BOSS. I think you do know, Bobby. Little Bob. My Boy. *(The BOSS leans in, confiding:)* You know, he's different than us.

BOBBY. Who, Max?

BOSS. You know. The college. The manner. The way he looks at things. I mean, he *is* one of us, but then again, he's not. Know what I mean? You and me, we're cut from the same cloth. You and me, we're one of a kind. Salt of the earth, y'know? But Max ... Don't get me wrong. He's a good boy, I like him, but, he's ... he's too—

BOBBY. —too jumpy?

BOSS. Exactly.

BOBBY. Well, maybe a little. But only lately.

BOSS. Lately?

BOBBY. Well ...

BOSS. What, then? Something wrong at home? His girlfriend's pregnant? His mother's sick? What?

BOBBY. Oh, I dunno ...

(Beat.)

BOSS. Bobby. I'd like to know if something is wrong. I'd like you to *tell* me if something is wrong with Max. Cause I realize something is wrong someplace. Somewhere down the line, things are going sour and it's my job to find out where the trouble lies. Now, I'm looking at you and I don't know. Is it with you? Maybe. Or is it with Max? *(Beat.)* Bob, I know how hard it is to talk about things like this ... but I think of you like a son, boy. You can talk to me.

BOBBY. Oh, I know, Boss. I know. You been real good to us. Real good. Like a Dad. You know, my Dad ran off with a telephone operator so's you're the only Dad I ever knew.

BOSS. Then talk to me, Bobby. Talk to me.

(Long pause, then:)

BOBBY. Max, he's a good guy, Boss. You know? We been working together for three years now. And—he's a good guy. I dunno. Somethin's eatin' away at him these days and I don't quite understand what it is. He's got some weird ideas all of a sudden and I don't know what's causin' 'em ... But he's a good guy, Boss. I want you to know that. He really is a good guy.

(Beat.)

BOSS. Bobby?
BOBBY. Yes, Boss?
BOSS. Would you like some Espresso?
BOBBY. Espresso?
BOSS. Yes.
BOBBY. Is that that strong coffee?
BOSS. Yes.
BOBBY. Tastes like Sanka, only you didn't add enough water?
BOSS. Yes.
BOBBY. Nah, I'm okay.
BOSS. You see this?

(The BOSS holds up an ornate espresso cup.)

BOBBY. What?
BOSS. My espresso cup.
BOBBY. Oh.
BOSS. Nice, isn't it?
BOBBY. Ah ... yeah.
BOSS. Very expensive cup. From Italy. Hand crafted. Imported from Italy.
BOBBY. It's nice.
BOSS. Not very many things are hand-crafted these days, Bobby. They're all made by machine. So when you find something unusual like this, you take pride in it.
BOBBY. I know what you mean.

(BOSS drops the cup. It shatters. BOBBY jumps.)

BOSS. Look what I did! It broke!
BOBBY. Oh ...

(BOBBY rushes to pick the pieces up.)

BOSS. No! No, leave it there. And *look* at it. Go on. *(BOBBY stares at the broken china.)* Do you see what we're left with now?
BOBBY. I think so, yeah.
BOSS. What are we left with, Bobby?
BOBBY. Broken pieces?
BOSS. That's right. It's no longer a nice, expensive, espresso cup, is it?

BOBBY. Well, if you want I could try and glue it back together—

BOSS. No! Oh, no, no. I don't doubt your abilities, Bobby. Don't think that for a minute. I'm sure you could glue it back together just fine. But what would we have then?

BOBBY. Your cup.

BOSS. But—it wouldn't be the same cup, would it?

BOBBY. Well ...

BOSS. No, it *wouldn't* be. For one thing, it would've lost all its value. It wouldn't be worth anything anymore. And for another ... odds are it would probably leak.

BOBBY. Oh.

BOSS. Mm-hmm. All over *me*, which would make me absolutely *livid*! *(The BOSS laughs. BOBBY does too, nervously.)* So. I guess we can't just take it and glue it back together, can we?

BOBBY. No, I guess not.

BOSS. So what do we do with it?

BOBBY. I dunno.

BOSS. Think.

BOBBY. Ah ...

BOSS. Think hard.

(Beat.)

BOBBY. Throw it away?

BOSS. Bingo! You're right on the money, Bobby! We throw it away! Bobby. Pick up the pieces of my cup and drop them in that garbage can over there. *(BOBBY must turn his back to the BOSS in order to do this, and this makes him nervous.)* Look what I found. *(BOBBY wheels around, expecting the BOSS to be holding his gun. Instead, the BOSS holds up another, less decorative cup.)* My old reliable espresso cup. Got it at the five and dime. Look. It's still intact!

BOBBY. Oh. Well.

BOSS. Would you pour some espresso into my dime store cup?

BOBBY. Ah.

BOSS. That pot.

BOBBY. Uh-huh. *(BOBBY pours.)* There ya go.

BOSS. Thank you. *(The BOSS sips. Pause.)* Ahhh. That's good. That's a really fine cup of espresso, Bobby.

BOBBY. Well, Thank you.

BOSS. See, I can use *this* cup. It suits me fine. Satisfies my needs. It may not be as fancy as the other one, but once the other one's in the garbage, what good is it to me anymore?

BOBBY. You got a point there.

BOSS. Exactly. *(Beat.)* Look. There's that fox again.

BOBBY. Oh, yeah ...

BOSS. You know, Bobby. If a baby fox were to venture away from its den ... if a baby fox were to make friends with us—with human beings—if he were to stray over here and make friends with us. If we fed him, took care of him, tried to make him one of our own ... when he went back to his family, you know what they would do to him?

BOBBY. No.

BOSS. They would kill him. They would chew his face off, eat his eyeballs out of his skull. Because the adult fox has a strong sense of family. Belonging. Where he belongs. Living inside a circle. That's how such an animal lives. And once the boundaries of that circle are knocked down ... you can't go back. Retribution, Bobby. Retribution must be sought. Do you understand?

(Beat.)

BOBBY. I think maybe I should go back to Floral Park.

(Beat.)

BOSS. I think maybe that would be a good idea.

(The BOSS smiles. BOBBY returns it. Blackout.)

Scene 3

(SETTING: MAX's place. That evening. MAX is frantically throwing clothes into a suitcase. A knock at the door. MAX draws his gun. Beat.)

MAX. Who is it?

BOBBY. *(From offstage:)* It's me.

MAX. Bobby?

BOBBY. Yeah, Max, lemme in.

(MAX cautiously opens the door, or, if there's no doorway onstage, steps off and comes back on with BOBBY. BOBBY stands there. MAX returns the gun to his shoulder holster.)

MAX. Are you okay?

BOBBY. Yeah.

MAX. You sure?

BOBBY. Yeah ...

MAX. Lemme see your fingers. *(BOBBY holds up his hands.)* Whew, that's a relief. I was afraid—

BOBBY. I know.

MAX. You know?

BOBBY. I know.

(Beat.)

MAX. So. C'mon in ... you want something? A beer, maybe? Some fruit cocktail? You got back fast.

BOBBY. You're packing, Max.

MAX. Ah, yeah. I'm—I'm packing.

BOBBY. Where are you going?

MAX. Ah ...

BOBBY. You going on a trip, Max?

MAX. Ah, yeah, I am, Bobby. I'm kinda—yeah. I'm kinda, ah, going on a—a trip.

BOBBY. You're leaving, aren't you?

MAX. Yeah. *(Beat.)* Look, Bobby. I'm sorry.

BOBBY. You don't have to be sorry, Max. You didn't do anyth—

MAX. —no, I did! I did! I told the Boss that—

BOBBY. —that I stabbed the wrong guy. I *did.* I *did* stab the wrong guy, Max. It's no big deal.

MAX. Look. Bobby. I gotta get going ...

BOBBY. I know you do.

MAX. Does the Boss know?

BOBBY. Know what?

MAX. That I'm going.

BOBBY. I don't think so.

MAX. You don't *think* so?

BOBBY. Mm-hmm.

MAX. What *do* you think? *(No answer.)* Bobby? *(No answer.)* BOBBY! WHAT DID YOU TELL HIM? *(Again, no answer.)* Did you tell him about the book?

BOBBY. No. Of course not!

MAX. *(Scared now:)* You're lying!

BOBBY. I am not!

MAX. Liar!

BOBBY. Max, I didn't tell the Boss about anything. I kept my word to you. *(Beat. MAX seems to relax a little, then:)* ... He just *knew.*

MAX. Oh my God ...

BOBBY. He's got, like, a sixth sense, Max. He knows when something's wrong.

MAX. I gotta get outta here ... Can I go, Bobby? Can I walk out of here?

BOBBY. What, are you asking me, Max?

MAX. Yes!

BOBBY. You're asking me if you can go?

MAX. Yes, I'm asking you! Can I go. Is it safe for me to go?

BOBBY. It's as safe for you to go as it is to stay, Max. *(Beat; MAX waits for an answer.)* Yeah, Max. You can go.

(Pause; MAX senses it's okay. He turns and reaches to close his suitcase. There is a glint, a flash of steel and suddenly BOBBY has his knife out and in his hand; he rams it deep into MAX's kidney from behind. MAX contorts in pain. BOBBY quickly grabs MAX's gun and holds onto it.)

MAX. Ahhh!

BOBBY. I'm sorry, Max.

MAX. "You're sorry."

BOBBY. I am! I really am. But, you see, I hadda do it. The Boss told me—

MAX. The Boss *told* you to do this?

BOBBY. Yeah. *(Beat.)* Well, In so many words ...

MAX. What'd he say?

BOBBY. He said you were a fancy espresso cup and then he broke the cup and said I hadda get rid of it. Then he looked at me, y'know? And I knew what he meant. I didn't have to ask him. I knew what he meant ...

MAX. He breaks a cup and you take it to mean you should go kill me?

BOBBY. He made it clear, Max. I was afraid he'd break all my fingers or nail my balls to a tree!!

MAX. Oh my God ...

BOBBY. I'm sorry, Max.

MAX. Yeah. Well ... You got your Merit Badge after all, didn't you?

BOBBY. Don't say that, Max ...

MAX. I guess—I guess you'll take my spot now, eh?

BOBBY. I'm sorry, Max. I'm—I'm sorry.

MAX. *(Spasm of pain, then:)* I was gonna get out ...

BOBBY. I know.

MAX. I was gonna have a *life*, Bobby ...

BOBBY. I'm not happy about this, Max. I want you to know, I'm not happy.

MAX. Then why'd you do it, Bobby? Huh? *(No answer.)* Listen. I'm gonna leave you with something, Bobby ...

BOBBY. *(Warily.)* Yeah?

MAX. I'm gonna leave you with my *ideas*.

BOBBY. No.

MAX. Maybe you'll write your *own* book.

BOBBY. Max, listen—

MAX. Maybe you will! You'll wake up one of these nights and *you'll* hear the voices!

BOBBY. Max. Stop it!

MAX. No matter where you go ... they'll follow you.

BOBBY. No.

MAX. Like they've followed me!

BOBBY. Stop it!

MAX. They will!

BOBBY. I won't let 'em.

MAX. *(Laughing weakly:)* You won't let them?

BOBBY. No.

MAX. You won't ... let them.

BOBBY. That's what I said!!

MAX. *(Mean:)* You just try and stop 'em!

BOBBY. You don't scare me, Max. You think you can scare me? Yeah, yeah, you think you're so smart, you got all the answers, but you don't. You never did!

MAX. And you ... you're just a garbage man, Bobby. A garbage man from Floral Park ... That's all you ever *were* and that's all—

(BOBBY stabs MAX again. MAX falls to the floor, dies. BOBBY leans against something to catch his breath. Long silence as his breathing stills. He wipes the prints off MAX's gun, replaces it in his shoulder holster. Take a lot of time with all of this. Gradually, the lights dim. BOBBY notices this and reacts to it. It's like some sort of supernatural occurrence ... BOBBY shrugs it off and turns to go. Then he hears it. A faint scream, barely audible, almost a hallucination, as if far away. He stops, turns around and stares at MAX's body. He is fearful at first, then a flood of bravado washes over him and he walks over to MAX.)

BOBBY. You think I'm afraid of you? Huh? I'm not afraid. You hear me? I'm not afraid!!

(BOBBY kicks MAX's body. Then once again. He kicks MAX several times, until he is satisfied that MAX is dead. BOBBY waits for a few moments, until all is quiet and still. He catches his breath, then turns to go. That's when he begins to hear them. The voices. One at first, then another. And then another and another ... they grow in desperation and volume, building on top of one another until it's a giant chorus of misery. BOBBY panics. He covers his ears with his hands, trying to shut the noise out. But he can't. He screams, totally consumed with fright. He continues to scream into the blackout.)

END OF PLAY

MEN IN SUITS PROPERTY PLOT

ACT I

Scene 1
train station bench
New York *Post*
briefcase
legal pad
fountain pen
jackknife (Bobby)
Grand Central Station
  train timetable
  signage (optional)
Scene 2
chair
coffee table/
  standing lamp
Scene 3
suggestion of Max's car
  (front seat of actual
  auto w/steering wheel)
Scene 4
IHOP signage
table & chairs
salt and pepper
  shakers (on table)
syrup dispensers
  (on table)
menus (on table)
small cardboard
  meal specials
  standee (on table)

cream container (on table)
sugar & Sweet n' Low
  packets in container
  (on table)
nail clippers (Bobby)
Scene 5
car (same as
  Act I, Sc. 3)
legal pad
fountain pen
Scene 6
urinal
comb (Max)
Scene 7
car (same as
  Act I, Sc. 3)
Scene 8
motel bed
motel nightstand
television (optional)
chair
phone
clock (on nightstand)
change (Bobby)
legal pad
fountain pen
briefcase
New York *Post*
Scene 9
Same as Act I, 8

add empty liquor bottle
publisher's letter

ACT II

Scene 1
diner counter
cup of coffee
spoon
cream dispenser
sugar dispenser
book manuscript
legal pad
Scene 2
white wrought iron
  lawn table
white wrought iron
  lawn chairs (3)
cigarette lighter (Bobby)
cigarette lighter (Max)
package of cigarettes
  (Bobby)
espresso cup (1 must be
  "fixed" to break each
  performance)
pot of espresso
wastebasket
Scene 3
Same as Act I, Sc. 1
add suitcase and
  clothes

MEN IN SUITS COSTUME PLOT

ACT I

Scene 1
Max— 2-piece
  suit with tie &
  dress shirt; shoulder
  holster & gun
Bobby—3-piece
  suit with tie and
  dress shirt
Scene 2
Bobby—jacket off,
  tie loosened
Scene 3
Same as Act I, Sc.1
Scene 4
Same as Act I, Sc. 2
Scene 5

Max—jacket off,
  tie loosened
Bobby—jacket and tie
  off, vest unbuttoned
Scene 6
Max—add jacket
Bobby—Same as
  Act I, Sc. 5
Scene 7
Same as Act I, Sc. 5
Scene 8
Max—same as Act I,
  Sc. 5
Bobby—suitpants and
  shirt only
Scene 9
Same as Act I, Sc. 8

ACT II

Scene 1
Max—same as Act I, Sc.6
Bobby—same as Act I,Sc 2
Scene 2
Max—same as Act I,Sc. 1
Bobby—same as Act I,Sc.1
Boss—cardigan sweater w/
  dress slacks and dress shirt;
  shoulder holster & gun over
  cardigan
Scene 3
Max—suit pants and shirt
  w/sleeves rolled up;
  blood pack
Bobby—same as Act I, Sc.1

ANY FRIEND OF PERCY D'ANGELINO IS A FRIEND OF MINE

CHARACTERS

FRANKIE, late 50's, a Mob Boss

TONY, late 20's, early 30's, a visitor to
FRANKIE's Long Island estate

SHARON, 30's, Frankie's wife

SETTING

In and around FRANKIE's estate in Amagansett.

The present.

ANY FRIEND OF PERCY D'ANGELINO IS A FRIEND OF MINE was originally presented as a staged reading at the Westwood Playhouse in Los Angeles on March 28, 1994 under the auspices of the Patchett Kaufman Entertainment Theatre play reading series. The play was directed by Joe Mantegna, and the cast was as follows:

Frankie ....PETER FALK
Tony ....CHRISTIAN SLATER
Sharon ....JEAN SMART

ANY FRIEND OF PERCY D'ANGELINO IS A FRIEND OF MINE received its world premiere at the West Bank Café Downstairs Theatre in New York City on June 19, 1996, produced by Anita Adsit. The production was directed by John Pietrowski, with the following cast:

Frankie.. JAMES KISSANE
Tony ....THOMAS HUMES
Sharon ....COLLEEN KIM GERAGHTY

The lighting and sound were designed by Laura Haynes.

ACT I

Scene 1

(SETTING: Backyard of FRANKIE's Long Island house; deck chairs, etc.
AT RISE: FRANKIE sits in a deck chair, an outdoor umbrella covering him. TONY stands in the sun, wearing a suit and sunglasses.)

FRANKIE. ... Percy sent you?
TONY. Yeah.
FRANKIE. Percy d'Angelino?
TONY. Yeah.
FRANKIE. Sent you.
TONY. He told me I could drop in, yeah.
FRANKIE. Drop in?
TONY. I said, you know. I was probably gonna be in Amagansett, he said—
FRANKIE. So. You're on intimate terms with Percy.
TONY. I wouldn't say that.
FRANKIE. But he told you you should come and see me.
TONY. Drop in on you.
FRANKIE. Drop in on me.
TONY. Yeah.

(Beat.)

FRANKIE. So I would say those were pretty intimate terms.
TONY. Well, You know Percy.
FRANKIE. I do. I do know Percy.

(Beat.)

TONY. So then.
FRANKIE. So ...

55

TONY. Here I am.

FRANKIE. So I see. Would you like a Mint Julep?

TONY. A—?

FRANKIE. My wife Sharon, she likes minty things. We got, like, ten quarts of mint juleps in the refrigerator, I think they gone bad. Burns my tongue when I drink 'em.

TONY. Huh ...

FRANKIE. She makes them, see.

TONY. She—?

FRANKIE. In the juicer, you know. Juice extractor.

TONY. Oh.

FRANKIE. I bought her one a them Juice Extractors. Now I think I'm gonna shoot myself. Other day she comes in here, some kinda pineapple/mint/peach nectar drink. I say, I'd rather eat a can of dog food. I think she was insulted. Because, last night, we sit down at the dinner table? I look down at my plate, and at first I think it's some kinda hash. Chili. Whatever. I lift a forkful to my nose, to test it out ... it's Alpo.

TONY. My God.

FRANKIE. Or Kal Kan, one a those things.

TONY. Huh.

FRANKIE. But she ain't gonna be making no juice for awhile.

TONY. Oh?

FRANKIE. I smashed that damn thing into a hundred million pieces. Sit down, sit down.

TONY. Thank you.

FRANKIE. So how's Percy?

TONY. He's good.

FRANKIE. Looking good?

TONY. Looking real good.

FRANKIE. How's his eye? That thing with his eye?

TONY. Oh. It's ... better. I guess.

FRANKIE. He always hadda wear sunglasses.

TONY. Still does.

FRANKIE. That's a shame. Havin' your eye all messed up like that.

TONY. I know.

(Beat.)

FRANKIE. He still in prison?

TONY. Yeah.

FRANKIE. Gets out in 19—?

TONY. He'll be paroled in 2019.
FRANKIE. Ah.
TONY. Yeah.
FRANKIE. That's too bad.
TONY. Huh.
FRANKIE. Nice guy like Percy D'Angelino.
TONY. I know.
FRANKIE. Did you know him before?
TONY. Before—? Oh, no, no.
FRANKIE. You met him after?
TONY. Yeah.
FRANKIE. So you was in, too?
TONY. Me?
FRANKIE. Yeah. You was—?
TONY. I was. Yes. Actually.
FRANKIE. You was.
TONY. I was.
FRANKIE. For what?
TONY. I, ah ... I robbed a, you know, a convenience store.
FRANKIE. Convenience store?
TONY. Yeah.
FRANKIE. You don't look like the kind a guy who would rob a convenience store.
TONY. Well, you know. You get desperate enough ...
FRANKIE. Yeah, I know that feeling. *(Beat.)* What kind?
TONY. Huh?
FRANKIE. What kinda store was it?
TONY. Ah ...
FRANKIE. What, was it a Pathmark? 7-Eleven? What?
TONY. A 7-Eleven! Hah! How'd you know?
FRANKIE. Odds. I'm good at odds.
TONY. Percy told me you were big on the horses.
FRANKIE. Used to be. I don't get out so much anymore.
TONY. Aw ...
FRANKIE. People follow me. Y'know?
TONY. Follow you?
FRANKIE. Watch me. Wiretaps ... directional microphones ... I gotta watch every word I say.
TONY. Ah.
FRANKIE. You should, too.
TONY. I will.
FRANKIE. If you know what's good for you.
TONY. Oh, I will, then.

FRANKIE. Cause you never know. Three wrong words ... and BANG! You're in a suit and tie in Federal Court.

TONY. Uh-huh.

FRANKIE. The way they do business these days.

TONY. I know.

FRANKIE. Not like the Old Days.

TONY. Yeah.

FRANKIE. The Old Days ... there was respect for you as a person. As a man. And now ...

TONY. And now?

FRANKIE. ... Alpo.

TONY. Kal Kan.

FRANKIE. Whatever. That's why I got them guards down at the gate. You saw my guards down at the front gate?

TONY. They frisked me.

FRANKIE. Sorry about that. Guards. And attack dogs. *(Shrugs.)* You gotta be careful. You know?

TONY. Oh, I know.

FRANKIE. You hear me?

TONY. I know.

(Beat.)

FRANKIE. Well. I'm pleased to meet you, Tony. Very pleased to meet you. Any friend of Percy D'Angelino is a friend of mine.

TONY. Thank you.

FRANKIE. I mean that.

TONY. Thanks.

FRANKIE. No problem.

TONY. Percy said you were a, a very generous fella.

FRANKIE. I try to be. I try to spread my wealth around.

TONY. That's what Percy said.

FRANKIE. It ain't no fun, hogging it all to yourself. You gotta ... you know. Give a little.

TONY. Giving is good.

FRANKIE. It is good.

TONY. Very good.

FRANKIE. Is that why you're here, Tony?

TONY. I'm—?

FRANKIE. Were you hoping I'd spread a little wealth onto you?

TONY. Oh—

FRANKIE. Like toothpaste, spread my wealth—

TONY. No, no, I—

FRANKIE. Cause if you're a deadbeat, I'll kill you. Right here. I'll drown you in the pool. If you're some kinda deadbeat comin' around here to hit me up for some *money*—

TONY. Oh, no, no. Nothing like that.

FRANKIE. Percy was always hittin' me up for money.

TONY. Oh.

FRANKIE. He didn't mention that, did he?

TONY. No.

FRANKIE. He was always comin' around, asking for money.

TONY. That's too bad ...

FRANKIE. Not really. I just finally got tired of him asking me for money. I told him, I said to him, you got to earn what I give you. So we put him to work for us.

TONY. That's what he said.

FRANKIE. He did?

TONY. He did.

FRANKIE. Told you he worked for me?

TONY. He mentioned it.

FRANKIE. He certainly liked to talk, didn't he? Man, oh man, did Percy like to talk ...

TONY. Yeah, he does ...

FRANKIE. That's why he's doing time.

TONY. Oh.

FRANKIE. He liked to talk, we told him not to talk. So we had to create a little Drama around Percy.

TONY. Oh ...

FRANKIE. Is that what you need?

TONY. Need—?

FRANKIE. Drama?

TONY. Ah ...

FRANKIE. Or you need work?

TONY. Well ...

FRANKIE. Did you come here looking for work?

TONY. Well ...

FRANKIE. Because there *is* work, Tony boy. For a nice young guy like you. There's work. But you gotta keep your hands clean. Hands clean and your mouth shut. But there's work. If you do that, there is plenty of work.

TONY. What kinda work?

(Beat. FRANKIE breaks into a big smile.)

FRANKIE. Beggars can't be choosers, Tony.

TONY. I know, I know.

FRANKIE. The dog don't ask the master "give me Kal Kan today."

TONY. I'm sorry.

FRANKIE. If you want work, I'll find you work.

TONY. I do.

FRANKIE. If you want work.

TONY. I do. I think.

FRANKIE. You think?

TONY. I think so. Yeah.

FRANKIE. You didn't come here looking for work.

TONY. Ah ... no.

FRANKIE. You did not.

TONY. No.

FRANKIE. We've established that. So why did you come here?

TONY. Percy told me—

FRANKIE. Percy told you, you should drop in on me. Fine. Great to meet you. But every dropping in is for a reason. Every telephone call, every time I pick up the phone and dial it, no matter who I'm calling, the laundry to say you scorched the collar on my dress shirts, whatever. There's a reason. A reason for everything.

TONY. Uh-huh.

FRANKIE. So. What's your reason?

(Beat.)

TONY. You know what?

FRANKIE. What?

TONY. I'd really love one of those Mint Juleps.

(Blackout.)

Scene 2

(SETTING: The kitchen. TONY and SHARON.)

SHARON. *(With great concern:)* Too minty?

TONY. Oh, no, no. No. Not at all.

(TONY clears his throat.)

SHARON. Frankie thinks it is.
TONY. Well, maybe for some people.
SHARON. If you don't like mint, I guess.
TONY. I guess so, yeah.
SHARON. You can take some with you, when you go. I got, like, twenty quarts in here.

(SHARON gestures to fridge.)

TONY. Mmm. Thanks.
SHARON. You could fill up your thermos, carry it around with you.
TONY. Sure.
SHARON. Hot day like this.
TONY. Scorcher.
SHARON. You want me to?
TONY. To—?
SHARON. Fix one up for you.
TONY. One—?
SHARON. Quart of Mint Julep.
TONY. Oh. Well ...
SHARON. It's no trouble at all.
TONY. Maybe.
SHARON. You mean no.
TONY. No, I said maybe.
SHARON. Maybe pretty much means no.
TONY. No it doesn't.
SHARON. You say yes, you mean yes. You say maybe ...
TONY. Yes, then.
SHARON. You'd like a quart!
TONY. Yes.
SHARON. I'm so glad! I'll have it all ready for you when you leave. *(Beat.)* When are you going?
TONY. I ... I dunno.
SHARON. Are you staying tonight?
TONY. I'm not sure.
SHARON. Did Frankie ask you to stay?
TONY. Not exactly.
SHARON. Oh.
TONY. He said, we had some business to discuss over dinner.
SHARON. Ah. Then, you're staying.

TONY. I am?

SHARON. We eat dinner very late.

TONY. Oh.

SHARON. So if he invited you to stay for dinner, he meant for you to stay.

TONY. Ah.

SHARON. Yes.

TONY. Good.

(Beat.)

SHARON. You look familiar ...

TONY. Me? Nah.

SHARON. You do.

TONY. Me?

SHARON. You really do.

TONY. How could I—? I'm not somebody you'd—Nah ...

SHARON. I'm trying to place you ...

TONY. You know Percy?

SHARON. Percy?

TONY. Percy D'Angelino.

SHARON. The one with the eye thing?

TONY. Yes.

SHARON. I remember him.

TONY. He's an acquaintance of mine.

SHARON. Not close to you.

TONY. Well ...

SHARON. Otherwise you would've said "friend." You said "acquaintance."

TONY. He's a friend.

SHARON. Acquaintance.

TONY. Friend.

SHARON. Whatever.

TONY. Maybe you met me through him.

SHARON. Maybe. But he's in prison.

TONY. He wasn't always in prison.

SHARON. I didn't know him before he was in prison.

TONY. I didn't either.

SHARON. So how could I know you through him?

TONY. Your husband knows me through him.

SHARON. My husband hates him.

TONY He—?

SHARON. Well, not hate. Hate is a strong word, isn't it? I wouldn't

say *hate*. They *used* to be friends. Dear friends. Brothers, practically.
But ... well, you saw the eye.
    TONY. Ah ...
    SHARON. Did he take the eye patch off and show you the eye?
    TONY. No.
    SHARON. Mind you, I've never *seen* the eye, I've just heard ev-
erybody talking about it.
    TONY. God ...
    SHARON. You know how he got the eye.
    TONY. No.
    SHARON. You don't know?
    TONY. No.
    SHARON. Then I shouldn't tell you.
    TONY. Please.
    SHARON. I can't.
    TONY. Come on.
    SHARON. I shouldn't.
    TONY. Please?

(Beat.)

    SHARON. Frankie got really mad at him.
    TONY. He did?
    SHARON. Yeah.
    TONY. What for?

(Beat.)

    SHARON. You want some more ice?
    TONY. No thanks. What for?

(Beat. She stares at him.)

    SHARON. I *know* I've seen you somewhere before ...

(Blackout.)

Scene 3

*(SETTING: FRANKIE and TONY stand at the edge of a lake facing
    the audience, casting reels into the unseen water.)*

FRANKIE. Flies like these ...
TONY. Oh, yeah.
FRANKIE. They're great, aren't they?
TONY. Terrific.
FRANKIE. If we don't catch nothing with *these* ...
TONY. I know.
FRANKIE. You hear me?
TONY. I do.
FRANKIE. I'm tellin' ya.

(Beat.)

TONY. This is a great place you got here, Frankie.
FRANKIE. The house, 10 acres of land, and the lake. Not bad for a guy who started out in business selling taps.
TONY. Selling what—?
FRANKIE. Taps. You know.
TONY. Ah ...
FRANKIE. For your shoes, bottom of your—
TONY. Oh, yeah, yeah.
FRANKIE. Metal taps. You know.
TONY. Yeah. My grandfather had 'em on his shoes, it clicked whenever he went to the bathroom at night.
FRANKIE. He wore 'em to bed at night?
TONY. No, well, he went kinda crazy, see. He'd wake up at three o'clock in the morning, wet himself, and then put his shoes on, walk into the bathroom and just stand there. Really pitiful ... So, see, I kinda associate taps with Old Men.
FRANKIE. Taps were definitely an Old Man's accoutrement.
TONY. I guess so ...
FRANKIE. But, you see: I realized this.
TONY. You—?
FRANKIE. That taps were on their way out.
TONY. Oh.
FRANKIE. I asked myself, what are Americans, American People, what are they always gonna *need*?
TONY. I dunno ...
FRANKIE. Things come and go. Fads come and go. Stuff comes and goes. But what is the one thing Americans are always gonna need? *Always*?
TONY. I dunno.
FRANKIE. Cigarettes.
TONY. Ci—?

FRANKIE. Tobacco products.

TONY. Oh ...

FRANKIE. No matter how many times you tell 'em it's killin' 'em, they always want another smoke. It's a proven fact.

TONY. Proven?

FRANKIE. Yeah.

TONY. Really? Proven?

FRANKIE. Sure.

TONY. Where is it proven?

FRANKIE. I dunno, but I'm sure it is. Someplace.

TONY. Ah ... *(They fish in silence for a moment.)* So, you, you started out selling bootlegged cigarettes—?

FRANKIE. No, no, no, no. Watch. Watch your tongue, slick.

TONY. My—?

FRANKIE. We don't use words like "bootlegged," or "stolen," or "racket" around her. *(Whispers:)* Microphones ...

(Beat; TONY looks around.)

TONY. Out here?

FRANKIE. Maybe.

TONY. Out here on the *water*?

FRANKIE. Hey. You never know ...

TONY. Look. I didn't mean to—

FRANKIE. Forget it. S'no problem. You're a friend of Percy's, so it's okay. If you was some stranger, if I was telling all this to some *stranger* ...

TONY. Well ...

FRANKIE. You know what I'm saying? I'd be using you for *bait* right about now!

(FRANKIE laughs. TONY joins him.)

TONY. Ha-ha!

FRANKIE. But you're not a stranger. Are you?

TONY. No. No ...

FRANKIE. You are a friend of a friend.

TONY. Mm-hmm.

FRANKIE. That is what binds us together, my friend. That is the currency in our world. That is the one thing that separates us from the— *(A tug on his line.)* Hey, I got something ... I got ... *(Pulls it in. Nothing.)* Ahhhh.

(They cast again. Silence.)

TONY. How many times have you been indicted, Frankie?

(Beat.)

FRANKIE. That's a personal question, Tony.
TONY. I'm sorry, I just wondered—
FRANKIE. Mighty personal.
TONY. I'm sorry!

(Beat.)

FRANKIE. S'okay. I'll tell you. I'll reward your natural sense of curiosity. *(Beat.)* Nine times.
TONY. Nine—?
FRANKIE. *(Shrugging.)* Yeah.
TONY. Nine times in front of a Federal Grand Jury?
FRANKIE. Yeah. Fifteen if you count all the times I was a witness.
TONY. How'd you get off?
FRANKIE. I told the truth. *(TONY looks at him. FRANKIE smiles slyly.)* And I had good lawyers. The best lawyers that money could buy.

(Beat.)

TONY. You know, you're kinda a celebrity, Frankie.
FRANKIE. *(Glad of this but pretending to dismiss it:)* Ah ...
TONY. You are. In certain circles.
FRANKIE. Me?
TONY. Yeah.
FRANKIE. Nah.
TONY. You are.
FRANKIE. Well ...
TONY. New York *Post*? Front page every day of that last trial.
FRANKIE. People seem to be sympathetic to the position I get put in. They naturally root for the innocent guy, y'see.
TONY. I know. People like you.
FRANKIE. And you know, I like them.
TONY. They wanna know about you.
FRANKIE. What's there to know? Eh? I'm just a working man who got his start selling taps.

TONY. No, there's a lot more to it than that. A lot more. You know ... *(Beat.)* They're making a movie about you.
FRANKIE. What?
TONY. Yeah.
FRANKIE. They—?
TONY. Yeah.
FRANKIE. Who told you this?
TONY. I dunno, I—
FRANKIE. WHO TOLD YOU?
TONY. I dunno, I read it someplace, I—
FRANKIE. Read it? *(TONY nods.)* READ IT? *(Nods again.)* Making a movie about—? *(Suddenly furious:)* AIUTAMI, DIO!

(FRANKIE casts his rod into the water.)

TONY. Frankie, your rod—
FRANKIE. I HATE THAT! I HATE IT, I HATE IT, I HATE IT!
TONY. Whoa, Frankie, I'm sorry, I—
FRANKIE. I HATE HOLLYWOOD! IT MAKES THE BILE RISE UP OUTTA MY BELLY AND MOVE INTO THE BACK A MY THROAT JUST TO THINK ABOUT IT!
TONY. Easy, take it—
FRANKIE. Coppola, at least he gave us dignity. Scorcese gave us class. But most a that garbage ... MARRIED TO THE—Non è vero? Huh? You hear what I'm saying? *(Utter disdain:)* COOKIE ... MOB-STERS, for cryin' out loud! Dannazione! What, I'm gonna be some stupid TV-Movie? I'm gonna—? What? What? What?

(Pause.)

TONY. Frankie, You threw your rod and reel in the lake.

(Pause. FRANKIE looks at the water, realizes he has indeed done this.)

FRANKIE. Oh ...
TONY. You want me to go in after it?
FRANKIE. No, no, it's okay ...
TONY. I'll go in after it—
FRANKIE. It's okay. Water's cold. I'll buy a new one. *(Silence.)* I want to know about this movie.
TONY. I really don't know anything more than—
FRANKIE. I want to know.

(FRANKIE starts up to the house.)

TONY. Where are you going?
FRANKIE. To make some phone calls.

(FRANKIE stalks out. TONY looks out at the water, looks at his rod and reel. Blackout.)

Scene 4

(SETTING: Front seat of FRANKIE's car. TONY sits beside him. FRANKIE gestures to things as he drives.)

FRANKIE. See those tulips? I planted those.
TONY. Beautiful. This is a beautiful driveway. Where are we going?
FRANKIE. Look! One a the attack dogs. He's found a bird. *(FRANKIE slows down, looks out the window intently.)* Watch. He's eatin' him alive ...
TONY. Mmmm.
FRANKIE. Those dogs, they're a lotta fun.
TONY. I guess so.
FRANKIE. We used to have this old man, the gardener? We sicked one a the dogs on him one day for a few laughs!

(TONY is appropriately horrified by this.)

TONY. My God! You—?
FRANKIE. Just kidding!

(FRANKIE bursts into laughter.)

TONY. *(Flood of relief:)* Oh ...
FRANKIE. I had ya there! *(Pointing as he drives:)* Wave to the guards. *(They do.)* At last. Open road!
TONY. Where are we going?
FRANKIE. I pay them fellas fifty grand a year. Not bad, eh?
TONY. No, no ...
FRANKIE. Considering all they gotta do is stand out there an scare people away.
TONY. Yeah.

FRANKIE. One day *People* magazine or one a them things, they showed up here. Tried to get in to see me.

TONY. Yeah?

FRANKIE. I wouldn't have no part of that.

TONY. Why not?

FRANKIE. Same reason I hate the movies. They take what you are and they turn you into something else. For their own benefit. Their own gain. I hate that.

TONY. That's America.

FRANKIE. That is *not* America. That's ... well, maybe you're right. Maybe it is. But I'll tell you one thing:

TONY. What?

FRANKIE. This movie you told me about?

TONY. Yeah?

FRANKIE. It will not be made.

TONY. Why?

FRANKIE. Because. I don't *want* it made.

TONY. But they want to do it right! At least, from what I heard. Read. Whatever. I was under the impression they wanted it to be a true portrait of you.

FRANKIE. It could never be a true portrait.

TONY. If research was done, if—

FRANKIE. Never.

TONY. Why not?

FRANKIE. Because. It's the nature of their business. They can't be truthful, no matter how hard they try.

TONY. I don't think so, Frankie ...

FRANKIE. Name one movie that was totally truthful.

TONY. Ah ...

FRANKIE. Did not compromise itself in any way.

TONY. Ah ... *(Beat.)* I dunno. Let me think ...

FRANKIE. You can think all night, you won't come up with one. I promise you.

TONY. Where are we going?

FRANKIE. 7-Eleven. I need some cash! *(FRANKIE laughs. TONY tries to join him.)* Where was that 7-Eleven. anyway?

TONY. Which 7-Eleven?

FRANKIE. The one you robbed.

TONY. Oh, ah ... I can't remember.

FRANKIE. Can't remember?

TONY. Ah ...

FRANKIE. Wait a minute, wait a minute. The only robbery you ever pulled and you can't remember?

TONY. Ah ... Queens. Or, maybe it was Brooklyn ...

FRANKIE. When?

TONY. Excuse me?

FRANKIE. When was this?

TONY. Long time ago.

FRANKIE. Couldn't a been that long. You're not exactly an octo-genarian.

TONY. Ah, well, my memory, you know, it's not so good.

FRANKIE. I see that.

TONY. Yeah.

FRANKIE. You gotta work on that.

TONY. What?

FRANKIE. Your memory. If you want a job.

TONY. Oh.

FRANKIE. One of my requirements is a good memory.

TONY. Yes.

(FRANKIE pulls up to a stop. TONY looks up to see where they are. FRANKIE starts laughing.)

FRANKIE. We need a quart of milk!

TONY. In here?

FRANKIE. Yeah.

TONY. A 7-Eleven!

FRANKIE. Yeah.

TONY. All you want is a quart of milk.

FRANKIE. Yeah. *(FRANKIE hands him a gun.)* And the contents of the cash register.

(Beat.)

TONY. You're not serious.

FRANKIE. I'm very serious.

TONY. Ah ...

FRANKIE. If you were to work for me, I can assure you your day would be a lot more hazardous than this.

TONY. Yes.

FRANKIE. Hitting some pimply-faced kid up for $200. Look. He's some stupid pimply-faced kid.

TONY. Ah ...

FRANKIE. You wanna work for me?

TONY Yeah.

FRANKIE. You gotta prove yourself.

(Beat.)

TONY. Right ...
FRANKIE. I mean, you already got an "in," you know Percy.
TONY. Yes.
FRANKIE. That got you in the front gate.
TONY. Uh-huh.
FRANKIE. This is what gets you the job.
TONY. Okay.
FRANKIE. You do want a job, don't you?
TONY. Yes.
FRANKIE. You said you were interested in work.
TONY. Uh-huh.
FRANKIE. So?
TONY. So?
FRANKIE. I'm ready to give you work. But first. But first. There's something *you* gotta do.

(FRANKIE offers the gun. TONY stares at it. Blackout.)

Scene 5

(SETTING: Dinner on the patio. SHARON, FRANKIE and TONY at the table.)

FRANKIE. My boy, my boy!
TONY. *(Mouth full:)* Mmmm ...
FRANKIE. Just like an old pro!
TONY. Well ...
FRANKIE. I dropped the glove, Sharon. You shoulda seen him. I challenged him, I dropped the glove today ...
TONY. I—
FRANKIE. ... and he—
TONY. Maybe we shouldn't be *telling* everybody!
FRANKIE. It's just Sharon.
TONY. I know, but still ...
FRANKIE. Hah! I love his modesty! You hear that modesty?
TONY. What if I get arrested?
FRANKIE. Tony! Tony, Tony, Tony. You're not gonna get arrested. Don't be such a baby.

TONY. I robbed a convenience store. I threatened a guy at gunpoint!

FRANKIE. And I'm proud of you!

TONY. This guy almost wet his pants he was so scared ...

FRANKIE. You didn't hurt anybody. C'mon. What, the 7-Eleven corporation *needs* that $486?

TONY. I know, but still ...

FRANKIE. Look. Tony. You don't have to worry about trouble. There will be no trouble.

TONY. How do you know?

FRANKIE. Tony. *(TONY looks at him.)* I *know.* I promise you.

TONY. Oh ...

(Silence for a moment.)

FRANKIE. I was beginning to have my doubts about you.

TONY. You were—?

FRANKIE. A little bit.

TONY. Oh ...

FRANKIE. I was beginning to think you were a Fraud.

TONY. Hah!

FRANKIE. But you proved yourself.

TONY. Yeah, well ...

FRANKIE. You certainly proved yourself. Here. You want more?

TONY. Mmm, no thanks. I got plenty.

FRANKIE. You like that?

TONY. Mm-hmm.

FRANKIE. Good, isn't it?

TONY. Yes.

FRANKIE. Sure beats Kal Kan! *(Laughs.)* I'm sorry, honey.

SHARON. Yeah, yeah ...

FRANKIE. She's a good cook, ain't she?

TONY. She is.

FRANKIE. Lotta the women, they don't cook no more.

TONY. No?

FRANKIE. Not anymore.

SHARON. I do.

FRANKIE. I'm just sayin'. Lot of 'em, they got servants. You know. People who do everything for 'em.

TONY. Ah ...

SHARON. More peas?

TONY. No, thank you.

SHARON. Another Mint Julep?

TONY. No, thanks.

(Beat.)

FRANKIE. It's nice having you here, Tony.
TONY. Thank you.
FRANKIE. Nice.
TONY. I'm glad to be here.
FRANKIE. Brings back old times.
TONY. Yeah?
FRANKIE. Mm-hmm. Kinda reminds me a little bit of Percy.
TONY. Huh.
FRANKIE. And you know?
TONY. What?
FRANKIE. All this talk about Percy ...
TONY. Yeah?
FRANKIE. Well, it kinda got me to thinking about him.
TONY. It did?
FRANKIE. Mm-hmm.
TONY. Oh.
FRANKIE. And I just thought ... I would love to say hi to Percy.
TONY. Huh.
FRANKIE. I really would.
TONY. Well, he sure is great to talk to.
FRANKIE. Isn't he!
TONY. Great.
FRANKIE. I miss talking to Percy.
TONY. I know.
FRANKIE. I really do.
TONY. Me too.
FRANKIE. You know what I think we oughtta do?
TONY. No.
FRANKIE. Guess.
TONY. I dunno.
FRANKIE. Try and guess.
TONY. I dunno.
FRANKIE. I think we oughtta call him up.
TONY. What?
FRANKIE. Since we're both buddies of his.
TONY. Ah ...
FRANKIE. Surprise the hell outta him! Let's give him a call.
TONY. We can't call him!
FRANKIE. Sure we can.

TONY. He's in prison!
FRANKIE. So? They got phones in there.
TONY. But they won't let him talk.
FRANKIE. Sure they will. If I tell 'em it's me.
TONY. They will?
FRANKIE. You know how many state officials I got on the—Oops!

(FRANKIE and SHARON laugh.)

SHARON. Gotta watch those bugs.
FRANKIE. Those directional microphones!
TONY. Ha-ha ...
FRANKIE. They'll put me through. I'm sure of it.
TONY. Yeah, but I, I hate to bother him.
FRANKIE. Bother him? Like, he's really busy! He's got a hot date tonight!

(FRANKIE and SHARON laugh.)

TONY. You know.
FRANKIE. No, I don't know. Tell me, Tony.

(Beat.)

TONY. I dunno ... I just hate to, to make him think too much about the Outside. You know. Gets him all stirred up.
FRANKIE. Stirred up?
TONY. You know.
FRANKIE. I don't think I would stir him up.
TONY. Well ...
FRANKIE. I just wanna say hello.
TONY. Yeah ...?
FRANKIE. Have a friendly little chat.
TONY. Hmm.
FRANKIE. Hear about his *eye*.

(Beat.)

TONY. You know. I really should get going.
SHARON. Going? You just got here!
TONY. I feel like I'm putting you out.
SHARON. Not at all. Eat!
TONY. No, I do. I feel like—

SHARON. Sit down and finish your dinner. We can talk. We don't have to call Percy right now.
TONY. I didn't mean that—
FRANKIE. No, no, she's right, she's right.
TONY. Huh?
FRANKIE. We don't have to call him now.
TONY. Oh.
FRANKIE. We'll call him after dinner.

(Beat.)

TONY. Look. I'm sorry, but I don't think it's such a hot idea.
FRANKIE. Why not?
TONY. Because. After what you did to his *eye*—

(FRANKIE looks at SHARON, who looks wounded.)

FRANKIE. You told him?
SHARON. No!
FRANKIE. You told him about the eye!
SHARON. I didn't!
FRANKIE. Dannazione!
SHARON. Frankie—
FRANKIE. A guy has his hand in the till, he's gotta answer to me! Percy was a good guy who went sour and he hadda answer to me! I hadda send a message! I—*(Stops himself.)* Did they sweep the place for bugs today?
SHARON. Yesterday they did.
TONY. I just meant—
FRANKIE. What? What did you just meant?
TONY. That maybe he's a little sensitive about you.
FRANKIE. Me?
TONY. And the fact that, you know.

(TONY points to his eye.)

FRANKIE. That's ancient history.
TONY. He's still sensitive about it.
FRANKIE. So sensitive all of a sudden!
TONY. I dunno ...
FRANKIE. *(Reaching for the phone.)* I'm gonna call him.
TONY. *(Rising.)* Excuse me—
SHARON. What are you doing?
TONY. I gotta—

FRANKIE. Siddown!

TONY. I gotta go.

FRANKIE. You can't.

TONY. I have to.

SHARON. You can't.

TONY. Why not?

FRANKIE. You gotta say hi to him.

TONY. I gotta go to the, ah—

SHARON. First door on the right.

FRANKIE. Stay here and say hi.

TONY. I'll be right back.

FRANKIE. If I get him on the phone, will you say hi?

TONY. I'd better not.

FRANKIE. Why?

TONY. He's—

FRANKIE. What's goin' on here?

TONY. He's mad at me.

FRANKIE. You?

TONY. Yes.

SHARON. Mad at you?

TONY. Yeah.

SHARON. Why?

TONY. I dunno ...

FRANKIE. This is stupid. If he's gonna be mad at anybody, he's gonna be mad at *me*, I poked his eye out! Lemme call him, we'll both say hi.

TONY. No!

FRANKIE. What is it with you?

TONY. I'm feeling ... sick.

SHARON. Too much mint. *(To FRANKIE.)* He had three of them.

FRANKIE. You're gonna feel a lot sicker in a minute if you don't tell me what's going on. *(Silence.) Some*thing's going on. Isn't it? Somebody sent you here.

TONY. No.

FRANKIE. You came on your own, then?

TONY. Yeah.

FRANKIE. For what *reason*?

TONY. I—

FRANKIE. See, we never got to the bottom of the reason!

TONY. Look, it's been great, really, it has, but—

FRANKIE. You're not going noplace!

TONY. Listen—

FRANKIE. You come in here, ask me about my business!

TONY. I—
FRANKIE. I don't know who you are!
SHARON. Frankie, I—
FRANKIE. I DON'T KNOW WHO YOU ARE!

(Pause. FRANKIE stares at TONY. Pulls out a gun.)

SHARON. Frankie—!
FRANKIE. I think you'll spend the night with us this evening.
TONY. I told you, I can't, I—
FRANKIE. I think that is what will happen.
TONY. Look, I appreciate your—
SHARON. Frankie, don't hurt him!
TONY. —kindness, really, I have always depended on the—
FRANKIE. Follow me.
TONY. What?
FRANKIE. Come on. Let's go.
TONY. Where?
FRANKIE. Just move.
TONY. Oh my God! You're gonna kill me!
FRANKIE. Will you just shuttup and *move*?
TONY. DON'T KILL ME! I ROBBED A 7-ELEVEN FOR YOU!!!
FRANKIE. I'm taking you to the guest cottage.
TONY. Guest—?
FRANKIE. And I'm gonna lock you in.
TONY. No, no, no, listen—
FRANKIE. Because I think ... here is what I think:
TONY. I can explain—
FRANKIE. —I think you're trying to take advantage of me.
TONY. You've gotta—
FRANKIE. I don't like it when people take advantage of me.
TONY. I'm not, I'm not, really, listen—
FRANKIE. I've heard enough outta you.
TONY. I'm not—
FRANKIE. Move! I'm taking you outside and then I'm gonna give Percy a call.
TONY. Please! Don't call Percy! He's gonna tell you all kinds of lies about me! He and I are not on good terms, he wants to get back at me, he's gonna tell you all kinds of—
SHARON. I know who he *is* now!
TONY. Wh—What?
SHARON. I *knew* I'd seen you somewhere before!

TONY. (Looking down:) Ah ...
SHARON. I knew it!
FRANKIE. Sharon, what the hell are you—?
SHARON. I can't remember your name, but—
FRANKIE. Sharon!
TONY. Please—
SHARON. Every Monday through Friday at two, right?
TONY. I don't know what you're—
SHARON. RIGHT?
FRANKIE. What *is* this—?
TONY. No, it's not—
SHARON. HE WAS ON MY FAVORITE *SOAP OPERA*!

(Dead Silence. All stare at each other. Blackout.)

END OF ACT I

ACT II

Scene 6

(SETTING: TONY alone in an empty room. Silence. TONY is seated in a chair, handcuffed to a radiator. After some time passes, FRANKIE enters.)

FRANKIE. I am trying to understand this.
TONY. I'm sorry, Frankie ...
FRANKIE. Don't. Call me Frankie.
TONY. I'm sorry.
FRANKIE. I am trying so very hard ...
TONY. What did he say?
FRANKIE. What did he *say*?
TONY. What did he say?

(Beat.)

FRANKIE. He is not a man of many words. As you *well know*.
TONY. Uh-huh ...
FRANKIE. He told me you came to see him.
TONY. That's true—
FRANKIE. Hey! I don't *need* you to tell me what's true. You got that? I don't *need* your endorsement! I don't need your—you got that? You GOT IT? *(Beat.)* Something about a interview ... Questions ...
TONY. Yes.
FRANKIE. Now it all fits.
TONY. What?
FRANKIE. This *movie* you been talkin' about. Sharon says she used to watch you on one a them soap operas. Had to do with doctors or something. You played a doctor.
TONY. Veterinarian.
FRANKIE. Yeah, well, I'm checking you out.

79

TONY. Listen—

FRANKIE. I'm checking you out, so just you sit tight for awhile. I'm gonna know what to do with you, soon enough.

TONY. I only wanted to—

FRANKIE. What? You only wanted to, what? Make a "buffone" outta me? Come out here and take advantage of me? That's what I get. For being so trusting. Sharon says I'm too trusting.

TONY. No. Listen. Lemme just tell you ...

FRANKIE. Oh, like you're gonna tell me something I don't already know.

TONY. Maybe.

FRANKIE. Hah.

TONY. I might.

FRANKIE. I'm sure.

TONY. I told you about the movie, didn't I?

FRANKIE. Well ...

TONY. You didn't know a thing about that 'till I told you.

FRANKIE. Yeah, well I'm findin' out a lotta things, believe me. And when I got the puzzle all put together ...

TONY. What do you wanna know? I'll tell you what you wanna know.

FRANKIE. I don't want nothing from you!

TONY. I'll tell you.

FRANKIE. I got my own people, I'll find out my own way.

TONY. It's called—

FRANKIE. I don't want you to—

TONY. "The Puppet Master," and—

FRANKIE. Wait a minute, wait, wait, wait, wait a minute. *(Beat.)* The what?

TONY. The ... "Puppet Master."

FRANKIE. That's what I thought you said. And just who is this Puppet Master?

TONY. Ah ... well, you.

FRANKIE. Me?

TONY. Yeah.

FRANKIE. What kind of a name is *that*?

TONY. I dunno; I didn't *write* it.

FRANKIE. Oh, you're just *in* it.

TONY. Yeah ...

FRANKIE. You're just gonna be dressed up in a three-piece suit playin' Joey Guccioni.

TONY. Ah ... no.

FRANKIE. Oh, you're the heroic D.A. who just can't make the case stick!

TONY. No.
FRANKIE. You're the noble turncoat Andrew Peretti.
TONY. No.

(Long pause. FRANKIE stares at TONY. Realization sinks in.)

FRANKIE. No!
TONY. Yes.
FRANKIE. Oh my God ...
TONY. That's what I was tryin' to tell you.
FRANKIE. I think I'm gonna be sick.
TONY. That's why I wanted to come out here and *talk* to you.
FRANKIE. I can feel the *bile* rising up in my throat ...
TONY. To *see* you.
FRANKIE. I think somebody's gonna die here tonight.
TONY. I wanted to make it *real!*

(Beat.)

FRANKIE. Real?
TONY. Yeah.
FRANKIE. REAL?
TONY. Yeah ...
FRANKIE. Oh my God ... Sharon? SHARON!
TONY. Look, I didn't come out here with any bad motives!
FRANKIE. No, no, of course not! You just lied to me and made me look like at total idiot!
TONY. I didn't mean to! I'm sorry! I just wanted to—
FRANKIE. *Nobody* makes me look like an idiot! You got that? Nobody!

(SHARON enters.)

SHARON. Yes, Frankie?
FRANKIE. You're gonna love this. This guy? Your pretty boy from the doctor show? Guess what his next great role is gonna be?
SHARON. I don't—
FRANKIE. Guess.
SHARON. Ah ...
FRANKIE. I'll give you three guesses: one, he's been eatin' dog food for the past two weeks; two, the bile is just about rising in his throat right about now, three— *(SHARON's mouth drops open and she points at FRANKIE with a quizzical, mouth-open look.)* Yeah.

(SHARON begins to laugh. She laughs for some time. Then,)

SHARON. That is so funny!
FRANKIE. It is, isn't it?
SHARON. My God. I mean, look at the two of you. He's so—

(Beat.)

FRANKIE. What?
SHARON. Nothing.
FRANKIE. No, he's what is he?
SHARON. I can't remember what I was gonna say—   .
FRANKIE. Oh, you can't, huh? You, who always knows the perfect words?
SHARON. Frankie—
FRANKIE. Oh, I see, I see, I see.
SHARON. What?
FRANKIE. You like his looks better'n mine.
SHARON. No!
FRANKIE. Mr. Hollywood here ...
SHARON. Frankie!
FRANKIE. Yeah. I see now ...
SHARON. See what?
FRANKIE. Drooling over him in that soap opera.
SHARON. I never drooled over him ...
FRANKIE. You're probably tickled pink to have him here.
SHARON. No!
FRANKIE. Hollywood has Come to Amagansett! I'm gonna have a heart attack before this night is out! I swear to God, I'm not gonna be the *only* one eatin' dog food around here!

(FRANKIE stalks out. Beat.)

TONY. I guess he's pretty mad, eh?
SHARON. I would say so.
TONY. Was he this mad when he busted up your juicer?
SHARON. Not this mad, no.
TONY. What do you think he's gonna do?
SHARON. I don't know.
TONY. *(Trying to laugh:)* He's not gonna kill me, is he?
SHARON. *(Not laughing:)* I don't know.

(Beat.)

TONY. Boy oh boy ...

SHARON. Yeah.

TONY. My acting coach said it was, you know. Good to get out there and do some *research*.

SHARON. Hmmm.

TONY. God! I don't know what the hell I was *thinking*.

SHARON. I dunno ...

TONY. I mean, you know. Would it have been better if I'd just told him up front, if I'd just said, "hi, I'm an actor and I wanna talk to you?"

SHARON. He'd've probably beat you until you couldn't stand up.

TONY. Oh ...

SHARON. Broken your nose or something. So you couldn't—

TONY. What?

SHARON. You know, *star* in nothing no more.

TONY. Ah.

SHARON. He hates Hollywood. The whole *idea* of Hollywood.

TONY. He told me.

(Beat.)

SHARON. Look. I know this is probably a bad time, but ...

TONY. What?

SHARON. I feel so stupid asking ...

TONY. What, what?

SHARON. Could I have your autograph?

TONY. My—?

SHARON. You don't have to, I just—

TONY. You want my autograph?

SHARON. Well, yeah.

TONY. You really want my autograph?

SHARON. Yes.

TONY. Okay ... *(She gives him a pen and paper. Handcuffed, he writes with some difficulty.)* There.

SHARON. Thank you.

TONY. You're welcome.

SHARON. For what it's worth, I always thought you were very good.

TONY. Really? On the soap, you mean?

SHARON. On everything. I saw your movies, too.

TONY. I only made two.

SHARON. I know. I saw them. I rented them.

TONY. And you liked me?

SHARON. Oh, I thought you were wonderful!

TONY. Gee ...

SHARON. Especially that one you did, you know, the thing in the Rain Forest? The adventure movie.

TONY. Oh, yeah.

SHARON. I liked that one.

TONY. Yeah. She was good, too.

SHARON. I liked her.

TONY. She got her start in the theatre. Well, I did, too. Yeah. That was good. (Beat.) It's nice to know I have a, a fan in Amagansett.

SHARON. You know.

TONY. What?

SHARON. Maybe if you showed him.

TONY. If I—?

SHARON. Acted for him. You know. He'd see—

TONY. I don't think he'd go for that. *(Beat.)* Do you?

SHARON. I don't know.

TONY. You mean, what?

SHARON. Well ...

TONY. Do a monologue for him? Or—

SHARON. Maybe. I don't know.

TONY. What if he hated it?

SHARON. If he really hated it? *(TONY nods.)* If he really, *really* hated, it, he'd probably kill you.

TONY. And if he loved it?

SHARON. I dunno.

TONY. Let's see what monologues I know ...

(TONY thinks.)

SHARON. I just always thought you were so talented. Maybe he'll see the talent in you too.

TONY. I know a couple of Shakespeare pieces. And a Neil Simon ... let's see what else ...

SHARON. Something funny?

TONY. Ah ...

SHARON. Or dramatic! Make it very dramatic, lots of yelling and all, so he can see a lot of acting going on.

TONY. Oh. Ah ...

SHARON. I think that's the key. If you can show him a lot of acting, he'll know you're good. And then—

(FRANKIE reappears. Stands in the doorway.)

FRANKIE. Gettin' pretty cozy in here.
SHARON. We was just talking.
FRANKIE. Uh-huh ...
SHARON. What're you gonna do with him, Frankie?
FRANKIE. I dunno.
SHARON. Oh.
FRANKIE. I haven't decided. The way I see it, I got several options: one, I could kill him. Two, I could maim his face with a bicycle chain so that he never got another acting job again. Three, I could feed him to the dogs; and four—

(TONY suddenly stands, booming out with a resonant baritone voice. The handcuffs make it difficult, but he does his best:)

TONY.
Blood hath been shed ere now, in' th'olden time,
Ere humane statute purged the gentle weal;
Ay, and since too, murders have been performed
Too terrible for the ear. The time has been
That, when the brains were out, the man would die,
And there an end. But now they rise again,
With twenty mortal murders on their crowns,
And push us from our stools. This is more strange
Than such a murder is.

(TONY finishes with a flourish. Silence. FRANKIE looks at TONY. Looks at SHARON. Blinks a couple of times. Leaves.)

TONY. I think he liked it. Do you—do you think he liked it?
SHARON. I don't know ...
TONY. I think I'm off the hook. What do you think?
SHARON. I can't tell.
TONY. Unless he really hated it. Unless he's going out there to get a shotgun or something ...
SHARON. No, no, I think he liked it.
TONY. You do?
SHARON. Well, he listened to the whole thing.
TONY. Yeah ...
SHARON. I think he liked it.
TONY. The power of the Theatre, Sharon.
SHARON. Huh?
TONY. To transform peoples' lives.
SHARON. I—?

TONY. That's what just happened here, I think.

SHARON. Yeah?

TONY. I *think.*

SHARON. Who's life?

TONY. His maybe? Mine? I don't know. But I think somebody's life was just transformed. In some way. It's like some religious rite, Sharon. The Theatre. The Theatre has this raw, primeval *power* ... to make us new again, to—Damn! I knew I should've done something Contemporary!

SHARON. Con—?

TONY. You know. Modern. Shown him I could handle some Modern-day dialogue!

SHARON. Yeah, but this was good.

TONY. No, it was wrong. All wrong. He probably didn't know what the hell I was talking about.

SHARON. Hey.

TONY. What?

SHARON. I got an idea.

TONY. What?

SHARON. You could go one better.

TONY. What?

SHARON. When he comes back.

TONY. Yeah?

SHARON. You could do *him!*

(Beat.)

TONY. Oh, no ...

SHARON. Yeah!

TONY. But if he hates it ...?

SHARON. Yeah?

TONY. —then that's *it.*

SHARON. Who says he's gonna hate it?

TONY. He can't stand me! I can tell! All that ranting and raving about "Hollywood! It rises up from my stomach like—"

SHARON. "In my throat."

TONY. What?

SHARON. He always says, "It rises up in my *throat,* like bile." *(Beat. TONY is wary. SHARON urges him on.)* "I hate that!"

(Beat. He looks at her, then joins in:)

SHARON and TONY. *(In unison.)* "I HATE IT, I HATE IT, I HATE IT!"

(Blackout.)

Scene 7

(SETTING: Half an hour later. TONY still handcuffed to the radiator, has his hair slicked back like FRANKIE and has one of FRANKIE's suit coats draped over his shoulders. SHARON stands in the corner of the room, observing him. FRANKIE stands in the doorway.)

FRANKIE. Che succede? Huh?

SHARON. Frankie—

FRANKIE. What is he doing with my suit coat on, eh? Did you—did you *give* him my suit coat? Che avete?!

SHARON. Frankie, just listen, will you—

FRANKIE. I don't want him wearing my suit coat. You got that, honey? Or do I have to pound it into your skull?

TONY. *(Blurting out, a la FRANKIE:)* I HATE HOLLYWOOD! IT MAKES THE BILE RISE UP OUTTA MY BELLY AND MOVE INTO THE BACK A MY THROAT JUST TO THINK ABOUT IT! Coppola, at least he gave us dignity. Scorcese gave us class. But most a that garbage ... MARRIED TO THE—Non è vero? Huh? You hear what I'm saying? COOKIE ... MOBSTERS, for cryin' out loud! Dannazione! What, I'm gonna be some stupid TV-Movie? I'm gonna—? What? What? What?

(TONY finishes. A stunned silence. TONY bows. FRANKIE just stares, open-mouthed. SHARON applauds. FRANKIE shoots her a look. She stops. Silence.)

FRANKIE. What ... was *that*?

TONY. Ah, it was—

SHARON. It was *you,* honey!

FRANKIE. ME?

SHARON. Yeah.

FRANKIE. THAT?

SHARON. Yeah.

(TONY nods in agreement.)

FRANKIE. THAT was supposed to be ... ME? *(SHARON and TONY nod. FRANKIE bursts into laughter, almost splits his gut. SHARON and TONY watch as FRANKIE laughs. TONY's confidence visibly fades. FRANKIE fights for breath:)* Wa-wa-wait a minute! That—that was supposed—? I don't sound like that! *(Silence. He stops laughing. SHARON nods tentatively.)* I DON'T! I talk like this: "Hollywood! Coppola, at least he gave us *dignity*! Scorcese, he gave us style!" I bite off my words with authority! But *this* guy ... he don't sound nothing like me at all. He's got one a them—what do you call it? Lisp! *(SHARON and TONY exchange confused expressions, as if to say, "No he doesn't.")* And the eyes? What's all that with the bulging eyes? Crazy eyes? I don't do that!
TONY. Yeah you do!

(FRANKIE turns to SHARON for help.)

SHARON. *(She hates to admit it, but...)* You *do*, honey.
FRANKIE. I DO NOT!
SHARON. When you get really, really ticked off sometimes, yeah, you do.

(TONY mimics the eyes again.)

FRANKIE. I DO *NOT* DO THAT! You look like some kinda Saturday Morning Cartoon! I—Why am I even DISCUSSING this? This guy is a bum and in addition to that, he's a bad actor!
SHARON. Honey, he—
TONY. Now, I take exception to that! At the Daytime Emmys, 1994, I won Best Actor in—
FRANKIE. LET ME TALK! *(Silence.)* When you finished the Shakespeare thing, I'll admit. I was moved. Okay? I was—The power of those *words* ... the *poetry*. Don't get me wrong, I like poetry, I'm not some Philistine ... And you delivered those words very well. The power of those words, the truth behind ... I left this room and I felt like you had held up a mirror to my soul. My heart. My heart and my soul. I went outside to my Cadillac. I sat down on the front seat. And I wept. Wept like a baby. For the first time in 20 years, I wept! I came back in here, and I was prepared ... I had made up my mind ... to give you my blessing. Let you leave. Give you and your movie my blessing. Because of the truth you had shown me here today. *(SHARON and TONY are greatly relieved.)* BUT THEN. I come back in here ...

and this! You throw this at ME? This—this travesty! I come back in here to embrace you and you make me look like a clown? Up there with my suit coat on acting like a clown? Bozo the clown! Is that what I look like to you? Is that—?

TONY. I'll work on it!

FRANKIE. The hell you will! I want my suit coat back!

(TONY tries to take it off. With the handcuffs, it's hard. He drops the jacket. It falls to the floor.)

TONY. Ah. Sorry ...

(Before TONY can reach for it, FRANKIE whisks it away, dusts it off.)

FRANKIE. *Now* I'm gonna hafta send it to the *cleaners* ...

SHARON. Frankie?

FRANKIE. What?

SHARON. I got an idea.

FRANKIE. Did I ask your opinion?

SHARON. It's not an opinion, it's an *idea*!

FRANKIE. God help me.

SHARON. No, now, you usually like my ideas.

FRANKIE. No I don't.

SHARON. *(Hurt:)* Yes you *do.*

FRANKIE. I do not!

SHARON. Well, you'll like *this* one.

FRANKIE. Uh-huh ...

SHARON. But, you gotta *think* about it. You can't just hear it and say "no," right away. You gotta, you know. Give it a chance.

FRANKIE. Sharon—

SHARON. No, now, *listen.* I'm gonna say it. And you listen. But don't say no as soon as I say it.

FRANKIE. Okay, okay.

SHARON. Think about it.

FRANKIE. All right.

SHARON. Cause you are always so quick to say no.

FRANKIE. *What is your idea already*?

(Beat; SHARON is proud of this and wants to present it well:)

SHARON. I think ... you should *coach* him.

(Did FRANKIE hear this correctly?)

FRANKIE. I should ... *what*?

SHARON. You know. Coach him. Help him out. Teach him all your little habits ...

FRANKIE. I am not gonna waste my—Habits? What habits? I don't have any "habits!"

SHARON. Yeah you do.

FRANKIE. No, I *don't*—like what?

SHARON. Well, you know, little *things*, that you *do*. Like you're always, you know. Like how you look at yourself in the rear view mirror every time we go out someplace ... how you're always yellin' at the dog whenever one a your business deals goes sour—

FRANKIE. Hey. I do *not*. Yell at the dog. That is my dog and I do not yell at him!

SHARON. Yeah you do: *(Imitating FRANKIE:)* "Ya hear that, lil' Frankie? I'm gonna make *meat loaf* outta you!"

FRANKIE. I have never said that to Little Frankie.

SHARON. Yes you did, I heard you.

FRANKIE. Listen. There is no point in arguing with you about this, because this is stupid!

SHARON. Why?

FRANKIE. It just is.

SHARON. Frankie.

FRANKIE. Enough outta you—

TONY. Frankie, you can't *stop* this thing from happening! This movie! You can't—

FRANKIE. You watch me!

SHARON. What, are you gonna handcuff everybody in Hollywood to a radiator?

FRANKIE. If I have to, yeah!

SHARON. Frankie. You can't see the forest for the limbs! You got a Golden Opportunity here but you don't recognize it.

FRANKIE. What are you *talking* about?

SHARON. You got the ability here to Fix the Race. You know what I'm saying? You could come outta this thing looking like the greatest thing since Hostess Twinkies. This guy comes to you, begging for your help. So why not *help* him?

FRANKIE. Because. I don't *help* people!

SHARON. It's in your own bested interests to help him—

FRANKIE. Sharon—

SHARON. —cause if you make *him* look good ... *you* look good. And that ain't a bad thing. Somebody else, Jack Nicholson, maybe, if he was playing your part, he wouldn't care what you think! But this guy ... this guy *cares*. Give him a shot. Cause if he comes through, it can only help you. *(Beat.)* I'm right. You *know* that I'm right.

(Pause. FRANKIE carefully considers this, then:)

FRANKIE. Okay. Look. I'll tell you what ...
SHARON and TONY. What?
FRANKIE. I'm gonna unlock you.
TONY. Thank you.
FRANKIE. But *first* ... first, you are gonna make a little phone call for me.
TONY. Phone call—?
FRANKIE. Yeah.
TONY. *(What else can he say?)* Okay.

(TONY waits for more information. There is none.)

TONY. To—?
FRANKIE. You're gonna call your movie studio.
TONY. Okay ...?
FRANKIE. And you're gonna ask them to overnight you a little package, care of this address.
TONY. What ... package?

(FRANKIE smiles, picks up a nearby phone, carries it across the room and hands it to TONY. Blackout.)

Scene 8

(SETTING: Outside; the table. SHARON and TONY are seated; FRANKIE holds a Federal Express overnight mail envelope. After the lights come up, he pulls the tab on the envelope, zipping the package open.)

FRANKIE. Your fate, my boy, is in the hands of the Scribes. *(FRANKIE removes a script from the envelope. Takes out his reading glasses and reads the cover page:)* "The Puppet Master, An Original Screenplay by Bill Phillips and E.M. Collins." *(Disgusted:)* Not even Italians ... *(FRANKIE turns a page, continues reading:)* "The

Puppet Master. Scene One. Fade In. Ext.—"
   TONY. Ah, that means, "Exterior shot."
   FRANKIE. Here, you read it to me.
   TONY. Me—?
   FRANKIE. Read it to me! Go 'head.

(For TONY, this has become the Pitch Session from Hell.)

   TONY. Ah ... "Exterior shot. Front Steps, Brooklyn Tenement—
Day. It is a hot summer afternoon in the year 1958. The first face we
see is that of 11-year-old FRANKIE. The boy is seated on the crumbling front steps of the building with his kid sister, ROSA. A baby
cries in the background. FRANKIE and ROSA watch as the body of
their father, Frank, is carried out to an ambulance, a sheet over his
head. He is dead. Cut to: Close shot, Frankie. A tear runs from his
eye and etches a path through the dust on his face. He turns to his
sister. She reaches up to wipe his tear away. He blocks her hand. He
is already tough, street-smart, strong, invincible. Frankie: 'Dad said
if anything ever happened to him, I was the man of the house'."

(FRANKIE points to SHARON.)

   FRANKIE. Now. You do Rosa.
   SHARON. What?
   FRANKIE. Do it.
   SHARON. What, do you see an Academy Reward on my mantel-
piece?
   FRANKIE. Will you shuttup and do the words!

(SHARON, pride wounded, reads.)

   SHARON. ... "You're just a kid, Frankie. You ain't no man."
   TONY. "'But I swear to God, Rosa. I will never let you and Ma
and my other five sisters go hungry. No matter what I have to do, I'll
do it. If I have to steal, I'll do it. If I have to kill somebody ... well,
I'll do that too.' Cut to: A MAN IN COVERALLS, who steps onto
the stoop."
   FRANKIE. You be the man now, Sharon.
   SHARON. What?
   FRANKIE. Do the—be the man!

(SHARON heaves a big sigh, reads on:)

SHARON. "Move outta the way, kid."

TONY. "Who are you, mister?"

SHARON. "Riverside Furniture. We're here to repossess the dead guy's stuff."

(SHARON gestures for TONY to resume reading.)

TONY. "The Man gestures to Frank's dead body. Cut to: Close shot, Frankie's eyes, as they flash. Something inside him snaps. He whips out a knife and stands in front of the man, guarding his doorway. Rosa screams."

SHARON. "Aahhhh!"

(FRANKIE takes off his reading glasses, ponders all this a moment. It appears as if he has a headache.)

TONY. *(His life truly depends on it:)* Well ... What do you think?

FRANKIE. Me?

SHARON. Yeah.

(Beat. FRANKIE thinks for a moment, then:)

FRANKIE. I think this is good stuff!

TONY. You *do*?

FRANKIE. Oh, yeah, this is *very* good, don't you think?

TONY. *(Flood of relief:)* Oh ...

FRANKIE. *(To TONY:)* Cause alla this really *happened*, you know.

SHARON. It did?

FRANKIE. Yeah.

SHARON. Your father died when you were 11?

FRANKIE. Yeah. And I hadda raise all my sisters, all by myself. They really researched all this, didn't they?

TONY. Oh, yeah. They spent *years* on it.

FRANKIE. *(Flattered:)* Yeah?

TONY. Yeah.

SHARON. I though you told me your father died when you were 22. And you had left home and you were making thirty grand a year—

FRANKIE. Shut up. *(FRANKIE flips through the script, finds another spot.)* Hey. This looks good, here. "Scene 20. Int.—"

TONY. Oh, that means, "Interior—"

FRANKIE. Yeah, yeah, I *know*. Here, go 'head, *read*.

TONY. Ah ... let's see: *(Reads:)* "Interior, Brooklyn Social Club - Day. A dark little hideaway filled with cigar smoke so thick you can hardly see your hand in front of your face. This is where the shady deals which fuel the Brooklyn Waterfront are made. The front door opens, and light streams in, fighting its way through the dense smoky mist which permeates every molecule of the room. A shadowy figure appears in the doorway. Cut to: A sign on the door which reads, 'Members Only.' The shadowy figure closes the door and advances into the room. We still cannot see a face, but suddenly a beam of light falls across the unidentified person's face and we see that it is Frankie, now age 18. Several older MEN sit at tables drinking vodka, wrinkles etched deep into their faces like so many cracks in ancient parchment. The room is dimly lit. Angle On - First Table. One of the men rises and faces Frankie."

(Again, FRANKIE gestures for TONY to hand the script to SHARON.)

SHARON. "Can't you read? That sign on the door says 'Members Only.'"

TONY. "'I want to talk to the Boss.' The men laugh. Deep belly-laughs. From deep within their guts."

SHARON. "And who should I say is calling?"

TONY. "Frankie pulls out a gun: 'Tell him ... Frankie's here.'"

FRANKIE. *(Bursting out in approving laughter, slapping his knee in delight:)* This ... is *excellent*!

TONY. Yeah?

FRANKIE. This is very good! Here, do that again, will ya? *Do* that: "Tell him ... *Frankie's* here."

TONY. "Tell him ... *Frankie's* here."

FRANKIE. No, no, no, get up. *(TONY does.)* You gotta learn how to carry yourself. Cause that's one thing you got problems with, is how you carry yourself. Watch, Sharon. You know what I'm talkin' about.

SHARON. Yeah, okay ...

(FRANKIE starts to walk. TONY watches.)

FRANKIE. Now, y'see? You gotta carry yourself with authority. You gotta walk like the King that you are ... follow along with me.

(TONY stays a step or two behind him, trying to imitate.)

SHARON. Wait a minute. Stop. Time out.

FRANKIE. What?

SHARON. That's now how you *walk*.

FRANKIE. What do you mean, that's not "how I walk?"

SHARON. It's not.

FRANKIE. I am just walking, like I always walk.

SHARON. No you're not.

FRANKIE. I beg to differ with you, your highness. But I *am*.

SHARON. No you're not, you're doin' somethin' different, somethin' weird.

FRANKIE. What?

SHARON. You're strutting.

FRANKIE. *Strutting*?

SHARON. Yeah. You look like a pimp. This is how you *really* walk.

(SHARON demonstrates.)

FRANKIE. You think *that* is how I walk?

SHARON. Yeah.

FRANKIE. That is ridiculous.

SHARON. Well, it's closer to how you walk than what you were doing.

FRANKIE. How can it be closer that what *I'm* doing? I'm *me*! Here, here, Tony, *you* do the walk. *(TONY pauses, not sure what the hell to do. He more or less does a burlesque of FRANKIE's version of the walk, looking like an exaggerated pimp.)* See now, *that's* good!

SHARON. He don't look nothin' *like* you!

FRANKIE. He's gettin' better, though.

SHARON. No he's not, he's gettin' worse!

TONY. *(Sotto voice:)* Sharon. Ahem. *Excuse* me. But if you don't mind—? *Frankie* likes it.

FRANKIE. *(Patting him on the back:)* That's right. Here. Do it some more. And say the line while you're walkin'.

TONY. "Tell him ... Frankie's here."

FRANKIE. Again! *Meaner* this time.

TONY. *(A scowl:)* "Tell him ... Frankie's here!"

FRANKIE. Now glad!

TONY. *(A smile:)* "Tell him ... Frankie's here!"

FRANKIE. That's good, that's good, see? He can do all the de-motions.

TONY. "Frankie's here!"

FRANKIE. Okay! Okay! *Now,* we're gettin' someplace!

TONY. "I'm Frankie."

(Beat; FRANKIE studies TONY a moment; then:)

FRANKIE. Lemme ask you a question.

TONY. Yeah?

FRANKIE. And don't, you know, take this the wrong *way* or any-thing. Cause you're doin' a good job here.

TONY. Okay ...

FRANKIE. What if I said I wanted to play my*self*?

TONY. *(His heart sinks:)* Ah. Well ...

FRANKIE. I mean, now that I think about it, how come they gotta get a guy like *you* to play a guy like *me*? Why don't they just ask me?

TONY. Well, see, it's like, they gotta have Stars.

FRANKIE. Stars?

TONY. Yeah.

FRANKIE. And *you're* a Star?

TONY. *(He always thought so.)* Well, yeah ...

FRANKIE. What if I decided I wanted to play my*self*? Eh? I think I might have an adaptitude for acting.

TONY. Well, these days, movies have gotta have Stars. To, to make any kinda profit back, you gotta have Stars in the picture to get people to go see it.

FRANKIE. People to go see it?

TONY. Yeah.

FRANKIE. You mean, people are gonna go out and pay good money to see *you*?

TONY. I hope so.

FRANKIE. Uh-huh ...

TONY. But it's not just *me*; this movies' gonna be filled with Stars.

FRANKIE. Filled with 'em?

TONY. Oh, yeah.

FRANKIE. Gonna be—?

TONY. Yeah. Filled, yeah.

SHARON. Who's playin' *me*?

TONY. You?

SHARON. I'm *in* it, right?

FRANKIE. She *better* be in it! Six years now, we been married, she better be in it!

TONY. Oh yeah, she's in it, she's in it.

FRANKIE. Ah! Now, y'see, Sharon. Sharon could play herself. I mean, look at her: she's beautiful. Isn't she?

TONY. Well.

SHARON. Aw, Frankie ...

FRANKIE. Course now, it wasn't always that way. When I first met her, her butt was about as big as a dump truck—

SHARON. HEY!

FRANKIE. IT WAS!

SHARON. DON'T TELL HIM THAT!

FRANKIE. WELL, IT'S NOT *NOW!* YOU GOT A GREAT BUTT *NOW!*

SHARON. Thank you.

FRANKIE. What d'ya say, Tony? Eh? You think we could at least get Sharon in it?

TONY. Maybe like, in a bit part or something. Like I was saying, all the lead characters have to be—

FRANKIE. *(He's catching on now:)* Ah! Stars.

TONY. Yeah. Major Stars.

FRANKIE. Uh-huh. Uh-huh.

SHARON. So then ... who's playing me? Am I in the script?

TONY. Oh yeah, yeah. About halfway through.

(FRANKIE picks up the script, flips through.)

SHARON. Hey!

FRANKIE. Lemme find it ...

SHARON. So? Gimme a hint.

TONY. Ah—

SHARON. No, no, don't tell me, let me guess: Michelle Pfeiffer?

TONY. Ah, no ...

SHARON. Melanie Griffith?

TONY. No ...

SHARON. Oh, I know, I know: CHER!

TONY. No ...

SHARON. Who, then?

TONY. Sharon—

SHARON. TELL ME WHO.

(Beat.)

TONY. Roseanne.

SHARON. What? *(FRANKIE bursts out with another peal of laughter.)* Shuttup, you! What is the logic behind something like that? A decision like that?

TONY. They wanted—

SHARON. My God! Is that how I *look* to people?

TONY. No, no, they just—

SHARON. How will I ever be able to look my friends in the eye?

TONY. No, no, you—

SHARON. Straight in the eye?

TONY. It was a choice that—

SHARON. Like, I *still* got a big fat *butt*?

TONY. Oh, no, no, not at all! They just—

SHARON. TWENTY THOUSAND DOLLARS' WORTH OF LIPOSUCTION AND I STILL GOT A BIG FAT BUTT?

(FRANKIE has found an appropriate page in the script:)

FRANKIE. Here, here it is. *(All gather around.)* "Scene 41. Interior Nightclub - Night. Frankie spots Sharon at the other side of the nightclub. Although he is flanked by half a dozen gorgeous blonde bimbos, he feels drawn to Sharon. She is heavyset—"

SHARON. Oh my god!

FRANKIE. "As she forces her way through the crowded room, her stomach palpitates like a mound of ungainly jello salad—"

SHARON. "Jello salad?" *(Grabbing the script:)* Lemme see that?

(SHARON reads.)

FRANKIE. Tony?

TONY. Yes?

FRANKIE. Lemme ask you a question.

TONY. Okay.

FRANKIE. How much does a movie like this cost to make?

TONY. I dunno.

FRANKIE. Take a guess. You're educated, and I would like an educated guess.

TONY. Eight, ten million I guess.

FRANKIE. Uh-huh ... And how much could it be expected to earn?

TONY. If it was a big hit?

FRANKIE. Big hit, let's say. For some miraculous reason, people actually fork over their hard-earned money to see it.

TONY. Big hit ... if it was *really* a breakaway hit ... well, like my last movie, it did pretty well.

SHARON. *(Reading:)* "Close shot on her *vast buttocks*!"

TONY. That one did pretty good.

FRANKIE. *(Skeptical.)* Uh-huh ...

TONY. I think it did somewhere in the neighborhood of ... eighty, ninety million.

FRANKIE. Eigh—? Eighty *mil*—?

TONY. Yeah, But that's only if it really hits. Otherwise the studio loses its shirt.

FRANKIE. This is kinda like the horses, eh?

TONY. Yeah. It's a gamble all right. You never know what's gonna hit and what's not.

FRANKIE. That's *just* like the horses!

SHARON. *(Throwing the script down.)* This is utterly disgusting! I want you both to know I am very, very upset! I will *not* have a butt which looks like jello salad up there on the screen for everybody to see.

FRANKIE. Sharon. Don't worry. I'm gonna fix this. I'll fix it. Don't you worry about a thing.

SHARON. You promise?

FRANKIE. I promise. *(He kisses her. Then turns to TONY:)* This movie. It's got a director, don't it? That's what you call it. A director, right?

TONY. Yeah.

FRANKIE. Uh-huh. So, what's his name?

TONY. It's, ah ... it's not a *he*.

(Beat.)

FRANKIE. What?

TONY. It's a *she*.

SHARON. Good for *her*!

(FRANKIE shoots SHARON a "shuttup" look. She does.)

FRANKIE. Lemme get this straight ... The story of My Life. The story of La Cosa Nostra ... a story filled with joy and pain and passion and suffering ... a story epic in its sweep ... this story ... is being directed ... by a *woman*?

TONY. Well, yeah.

FRANKIE. Who?

TONY. Ah ...

FRANKIE. I WANNA KNOW HER NAME!

TONY. I don't know if I should—

FRANKIE. NOW!

TONY. Penny, ah Penny Marshall.

SHARON. Ooh! She's good! She's the one, was on *Laverne & Shirley*! *(To FRANKIE:)* You remember. She had the "L" on all her clothes!

FRANKIE. What?

SHARON. Yeah!

FRANKIE. The woman with the "L" on all her clothes is directing the Story of My Life?

TONY. She doesn't *really* wear "L's—"

FRANKIE. GET HER ON THE PHONE!

SHARON. Frankie—

FRANKIE. NOW!

TONY. Ah, Frankie, the thing is—

FRANKIE. I WANNA TALK TO HER!
TONY. But, Frankie, no, y'see—
FRANKIE. *WHAT? WHAT? WHAT?*

(Beat.)

TONY. You can't just ... call Penny Marshall *up.*
FRANKIE. Why not?
TONY. Cause. She's a Star.
FRANKIE. Oh. She is, eh?
TONY. Well, yeah.
FRANKIE. So, what'm I? Yesterday's News? Gimme her phone number.
TONY. I don't have it.
FRANKIE. You're lyin' to me!
TONY. I don't!
FRANKIE. She's directing your movie and you don't have her phone number?
TONY. Well, yeah, I *do, (But ...)*
FRANKIE. So?
TONY. It's in my Dayrunner.
FRANKIE. Where's your Dayrunner?
TONY. In my briefcase.
FRANKIE. Where's your briefcase?
TONY. In my apartment.

(FRANKIE is at a loss for words. He lets out a frustrated scream to the heavens. A small dog begins to yap offstage.)

FRANKIE. Shuttup, Little Frankie! Shuttup, you stupid mutt! If you don't shuttup, I'm gonna make *meat loaf* outta y— (FRANKIE stops himself, looks at SHARON. Her face says, "I told you so." FRANKIE takes a few deep breaths, calms. Composes himself.) When's this movie start shooting? S'that whatcha call it? "Shooting?"
TONY. Yeah.
FRANKIE. When?
TONY. Ah ... a week from Monday.
FRANKIE. Where?
TONY. In, in Los Angeles.
FRANKIE. Okay. Well, there are a few "details" we gotta straighten out before this thing gets off the ground ...
TONY. Wait a minute. What "details?"
FRANKIE. I wanna make sure I get a fair shake. You know, come off lookin' good.

TONY. Oh, you'll look good, I promise you, I'll make *sure* you come off looking good!

FRANKIE. You don't see what I'm sayin'.

TONY. *(No he doesn't:)* What are you saying?

FRANKIE. See, like with any deal I make, I need certain assurances. *(TONY isn't following FRANKIE, who realizes this and explains:)* I'm gonna need to sit all them producers down ... sit 'em down, and I'm gonna need to *explain* a few things to 'em, right up front.

TONY. Whoa, Frankie—!

FRANKIE. What?

TONY. It doesn't work that way! These people will not sit down and *talk* to you!

FRANKIE. Why not?

TONY. They won't even return *phone calls*!

FRANKIE. Oh, yeah? Well, they'll return *my* phone calls if they know what's good for 'em!

TONY. Frankie, this isn't *The Godfather*! You can't stick a horse's head in their bed and expect them to run out of the house screaming!

FRANKIE. What?

SHARON. *(Remembering the movie:)* Oh, that was so gross!

FRANKIE. *(Realizing that perhaps TONY is right, another attack:)* Okay, okay, so then maybe there's another *angle* to this thing...

TONY.   SHARON.

Angle—? What're you—?   Frankie, what are you—?

(FRANKIE motions for SHARON to keep quiet.)

FRANKIE. ... I mean, hey: if some movie studio can put up eight million bucks to make this thing ... maybe I can too!

TONY. Ah ... ten. I said *ten*!

FRANKIE. All right, then, so I'll put up ten. I'll put up *twenty*! I don't care!

SHARON. Since when you got *that* kinda money?

FRANKIE. *(Looking at SHARON with another of his "shuttup" glares:)* I'll put up *whatever it takes* ... *(To TONY:)* But lemme just tell you one thing, Tony, and this is a thing I learned a long time ago: *I* run the show, *I* call the shots.

TONY. What are you talking about?

FRANKIE. *(To SHARON:)* Get us all a drink.

SHARON. What?

FRANKIE. You know.

SHARON. What kinda drink?

FRANKIE. I dunno, just get us one a your—whatever!

SHARON. *(Hopefully:)* You want a Mint Julep?

FRANKIE. I don't care, just get some drinks! Somethin'! We're gonna celebrate here.

(SHARON goes.)

TONY. Celebrate what?

FRANKIE. Me bein' your producer. I mean, hey. It's like when we used to highjack trucks.

TONY. *(Totally lost now:) What* is?

FRANKIE. You know: If they won't see things *my* way, I'll just take the movie away and make it myself! Hah!

(FRANKIE laughs proudly.)

TONY. *(Beginning to hyperventilate:)* What? What, you think—? Oh my God ... Frankie!

FRANKIE. Now, I can see you're getting excited ... Listen. *You,* Tony-boy, don't you worry. You been loyal to me. You, I'm lookin' out for. You, I'm gonna take care of. But I'll put the rest of 'em in their place. I'll show 'em. All those Hollywood types ...

TONY. You can't push a movie studio around! You'll never get away with it!

FRANKIE. That's what they said about the cigarettes, too, y'know. But that is why I have always *survived,* Tony. Because I am an adaptable man.

TONY. Frankie, come on!

FRANKIE. Come on, what do you mean, "come on?"

TONY. That was a long time ago!

FRANKIE. So?

TONY. *So* ... just because you used to sell stolen cigarettes out of the trunk of your car—that doesn't mean you can produce a movie! You don't know the first thing about—

FRANKIE. So, what is it I have to know to be a movie producer? Huh?

TONY. A lot! You have to know—

FRANKIE. I know about my *life*! S'more than this woman with the L's probably knows. What else? What *else* I gotta know?

TONY. *(Grasping at straws.)* I dunno, how the, how the whole *business* works!

FRANKIE. I already know how business works. I'm a businessman.

TONY. Not *this* business!

FRANKIE. Lemme tell you something, Tony. All businesses, all businesses are the same.

TONY. No, Frankie, y'see—

FRANKIE. Tony, let me give you a little Life Lesson here: your Life

Lesson for the day: it don't matter what the business is, the one with the most muscle is the one who wins. So you stand back, Tony. You stand back and watch. Cause I've got a lotta muscle!

TONY. I can't—Frankie, this isn't going to work.

FRANKIE. What?

TONY. I just—I can't let you *do* this.

FRANKIE. I'm gonna *do* what I wanna do, Tony.

TONY. No!

FRANKIE. What? What did you say?

TONY. I said—

FRANKIE. Did I hear you correctly? You said, "no?"

TONY. I have worked too hard—

FRANKIE. What, you wanna talk about hard *work*? You listen to me—

TONY. —to let you *ruin* this! This is *my* big break, Frankie!

FRANKIE. Oh yeah? Well this is my *Life Story*!

TONY. I am not going to stand here and let you turn it into some Mafioso Amateur Hour!

FRANKIE. You ungrateful little rat! I said I'd look out for you—

TONY. Frankie, I won't let you do this!

FRANKIE. You "Won't let me do this?"

TONY. You aren't going to mess it all up—

FRANKIE. —I just wanna get this straight here: You "won't *let* me do this."

TONY. No!

FRANKIE. *(Big smile:)* Tony ... *(Then, sharp as steel:)* Are you threatening me?

(SHARON enters with the drinks.)

SHARON. Mint Juleps for everybody!

FRANKIE. Did you hear that? He just threatened me!

SHARON. He did? Tony, you threatened him?

TONY. No, no, I was just, just saying—

FRANKIE. —after all I've *done* for you, are you—?

TONY. Stop it—

FRANKIE. —are you *threatening* me?

TONY. Yes! No. I mean ... *(Beat.)* Okay, look: they let me go! All right? My contract is up, and—I can't go back to the Soap, I can't go back to the Veterinary Clinic, Frankie! That is no longer an option for me! Do you understand what I'm telling you? This picture is my last chance, and if it bombs, it's all over! This movie is going to make or break my whole career, and I am not about to stand here and let you screw it all up!

FRANKIE. So ... what are you prepared to *do* about it?

(FRANKIE slowly and deliberately takes out a gun, places it on the table between them.)

SHARON. Oh my God ...

FRANKIE. I asked you a question: what are you prepared to do?

TONY. *(Staring at the gun.)* I ... I don't know.

FRANKIE. Are you prepared to kill for this?

TONY. I hadn't actually, you know, *thought* about it in those terms...

FRANKIE. You better be ready to put up a fight, Tony.

TONY. *(Trying to negotiate:)* Listen—

FRANKIE. Because I guarantee you, I will fight you!

TONY. But—

FRANKIE. Are you prepared to fight me?

TONY. Frankie—

FRANKIE. ARE YOU PREPARED TO FIGHT? C'MON, YOU LITTLE WOOS! *(FRANKIE shoves TONY. TONY does not strike back, but he does not back away, either. In fact, as the following builds, they will eventually wind up screaming at each other, nose-to-nose.)* 'CAUSE I AIN'T GOIN' NOWHERE, TONY! YOU HEAR THAT? THE ONLY WAY YOU'RE GONNA GET THIS MOVIE BACK IS BY USIN' THAT!

TONY. FRANKIE, NO!

FRANKIE. YOU HEAR THAT? YOU'RE GONNA HAFTA KILL ME IF YOU WANNA WALK OUTTA HERE ALIVE!

TONY. NO!

FRANKIE. I don't give up without a fight, Tony!

TONY. That's very admirable, but—

(FRANKIE slaps TONY.)

FRANKIE. YOU HEAR ME? ARE YOU PREPARED TO FIGHT?

TONY. FRANKIE—

(FRANKIE slaps TONY again.)

FRANKIE. ARE YOU PREPARED TO FIGHT ME?!

TONY. YES!

FRANKIE. TO KICK MY TEETH IN?

TONY. YES, DAMMIT!!!

FRANKIE. TO RIP MY HEART OUT AND STOMP ON IT LIKE A PIECE OF DIRT ON THE BOTTOM OF YOUR SHOE?

TONY. YESSS!!!

FRANKIE.	TONY.
THEN DO IT!! DO IT, TONY!!	YOU ASKED FOR IT,
DO IT! NOW!!!!	FRANKIE! YOU ASKED FOR
	IT! YOU—AAAAHHHHH!!!!!

(TONY lunges for the gun, grabs it and fires. Click. Click. It is empty. Beat. FRANKIE breaks out into a big, broad smile. Laughs. SHARON laughs too. FRANKIE steps forward and proudly pats a numb TONY's cheeks with his hands in a conclusive, triumphant manner.)

FRANKIE. *Now* ... you're ready to play me!

SHARON. *(Applauding:)* Oh, you were great, Tony!

FRANKIE. *(To SHARON, all smiles now:)* He has some backbone after all!

SHARON. I told ya.

(FRANKIE takes his glass. SHARON and a confused TONY do the same.)

TONY. You mean—?

(FRANKIE and SHARON look at each other and burst out laughing.)

FRANKIE. He's a gullible kid.

SHARON. But he'll be good as you.

(FRANKIE peers at TONY, as if sizing him up for the role.)

FRANKIE. Yeah, well ... look. *(Slapping TONY on the back, fondly:)* We'll give the woman with the "L's" a chance—But I'll be watching. And if she don't *deliver* ...(The thought is left unfinished as FRANKIE raises his glass in a toast.)* Salute!

(They drink. TONY and FRANKIE grimace at the taste of SHARON's Mint Juleps.)

SHARON. Too Minty ...?

(Blackout.)

END OF PLAY

Any Friend of Percy D'Angelino Is a Friend of Mine

PROPERTY PLOT

Scene1
Patio table & chairs w/umbrella
Scene 2
suggested kitchen setting
  (fridge and/or counter)
juice extractor
glass of juice
Scene 3
2 rods & reels
Scene 4
Frankie's car (suggested by
  2 stools or front auto seat
  w/steering wheel)
handgun (Frankie)
Scene 5
dinner dishes w/food
phone

handgun (Frankie)
Scene 6
radiator
handcuffs
pen & paper (for
  autograph)
Scene 7
radiator
handcuffs
phone
Scene 8
Federal Express envelope
  w/manuscript inside
reading glasses (Frankie)
handgun
tray w/3 glasses of juice

Any Friend of Percy D'Angelino Is a Friend of Mine

COSTUME PLOT

TONY
Scene 1 - suit & sunglasses
Scene 2 & 3 - same as 1,
  without sunglasses
Scene 4 & 5 - same as 2,
  without jacket
Scene 6 - same as 5, only roll
  up sleeves, strike tie (if
  wearing tie)
Scene 7 & 8 - identical suit to
  Frankie's

FRANKIE
Scene 1 - bathrobe & slippers
Scene 3 to 8 - nice Italian
  suit

SHARON
Scene 1 - house dress &
  slippers
Scene 5 - tight p ants and
  casual top
Scene 6 to 8 - slinky dress

FAMILY VALUES

VINNIE RAMPULO
ANN-MARIE, his wife
THE KID, a 6-year-old boy
THE BOSS
CHARLES, a tailor
DR. ROSENBAUM, a male M.D.
DR. McCAFFREY, a female M.D.
A **NUN,** played by the same actress who plays DR. McCAFFREY
SEVERAL MAFIOSI,
"made" men ranging in age from 35-60, played by the same
actors who play CHARLES and DR. ROSENBAUM

SETTING

The present.

Various locations in Queens and New Jersey. All of these locations are suggested with a set piece or two—a tailoring mirror and a rack of fine sportcoats for the clothing store, two stools and maybe a steering wheel for the car, a bed and a vanity for a bedroom, etc. Light and sound will play an important role in establishing all of these locations.

The play is designed to be played without an Intermission, but if desired, one can be inserted between Scenes 4 and 5.

No, the script is not littered with typos. Vinnie and Ann-Marie have a very "unique" way of phrasing things, that's all.

FAMILY VALUES was originally presented as a staged reading at the Westwood Playhouse in Los Angeles under the auspices of the Patchett Kaufman Entertainment Theatre Play Reading Series on October 18, 1993 under the direction of Dan Lauria. The cast was as follows:

Vinnie Rampulo	RAY ABRUZZO
Ann-Marie	KIM ZIMMER
Charles/Man #1	GLEN TARANTO
Dr. Rosenbaum/Man #2	RICHARD PORTNOW
Dr. McCaffrey	M. JENNIFER EVANS
Giuseppe/Man #3	LOU BONACKI
A Nun	MIMI COZZENS
The Kid	JUSTIN WINEGRED
The Boss	RICHARD ZAVAGLIA
Narrator	EMILY RUTHERFURD

A revised version of *FAMILY VALUES* was subsequently presented at the Egyptian Arena Theatre in Hollywood by the Grace Players on November 8, 1994 under the direction of Richard Kline. The cast was as follows:

Vinnie Rampulo	JOE MANTEGNA
Ann-Marie	NATALIJA NOGULICH
Charles	JOHN RODGERS
Dr. Rosenbaum	EARL CARROLL
Dr. McCaffrey	KATHLEEN WALKER
Giuseppe	EARL CARROLL
A Nun	GABRIELLE GALANTER
The Kid	TIM WALKER
The Boss	RICHARD ZAVAGLIA
Mafiosi	EARL CARROLL, PETER MELE, GABRIEL LIEBESKID

Scene 1

(SETTING: Wednesday afternoon. An upscale men's clothing store. AT RISE: VINNIE RAMPULO is being fitted for a fancy, fancy suit. He stands in front of a three-fold mirror, admiring himself. His wife ANN-MARIE chews gum and flips idly through a magazine a few feet away. She has hair piled high in common Queens fashion.)

VINNIE. Whaddya think? *(She leafs through the magazine, shrugs, does not look up.)* Hey! I ast you a question!

(Beat; she looks up.)

ANN-MARIE. It's good.
VINNIE. *(Beaming:)* Yeah?
ANN-MARIE. It's fine.
VINNIE. You think so?
ANN-MARIE. It's magnicitent, whaddya want from me, eh?
VINNIE. Hey! How many times we gotta go through this? Huh? Friday is an Important Day for me!
ANN-MARIE. *(Shrugging it off, going back to the magazine:)* Fffft.
VINNIE. How often does a guy get m—? *(He looks around, goes right over to her, whispers in her ear.)* How often does somethin' like this *happen* to a guy like me? Eh? *(She shrugs, keeps reading magazine. He moves back over to the mirror.)* Yeah, like you could give two shits. What a reciprocational relationship *this* is!

(She looks up.)

ANN-MARIE. A what?

109

VINNIE. Reciprocational.

ANN-MARIE. That's not a word.

VINNIE. Yes it is.

ANN-MARIE. No it's not!

VINNIE. I said it sarcasmically. It means: whenever you ask me an opinion about something and I tell *you.*

ANN-MARIE. Like what?

VINNIE. Like, I dunno, like—

ANN-MARIE. Like what?

VINNIE. I'm *tryin' ta think! (Beat; he thinks. She waits.)* Like ... your *hair.*

ANN-MARIE. My what?

VINNIE. Your hair. *(Pause. She stares at him as if his hair just turned aqua.)* The other day. You ast me "does this look good?" I told you, yeah.

ANN-MARIE. No you didn't.

VINNIE. Your highness, I believe I did.

ANN-MARIE. That wasn't the way it was at all!

VINNIE. Yes it was!

ANN-MARIE. It was not! That was just one incidence and that wasn't how it was at all—

VINNIE. One what?

ANN-MARIE. —You didn't compliment me, I practically hadda drag it outta ya!

VINNIE. That is bullshit.

ANN-MARIE. Think what you want.

VINNIE. Yeah, well, I know what I'm thinking, and I'm thinking what you just said was total bullshit.

ANN-MARIE. Think what you want.

VINNIE. I will.

ANN-MARIE. Fine.

VINNIE. Oh, and just so you know, "incidence" is not a word.

ANN-MARIE. Yes it is.

VINNIE. No; it's not.

ANN-MARIE. You've never heard of "*co*-incidence?"

VINNIE. Yeah.

ANN-MARIE. Okay then.

VINNIE. But "incidence" is not a word.

ANN-MARIE. What'd I just say?

VINNIE. Not by itself!

(CHARLES, a salesman of fine breeding, enters.)

CHARLES. Shall I mark the pants, sir?
VINNIE. No!
CHARLES. *(Turning to go:)* All right. Perhaps you'd like a few more minutes ...
VINNIE. Hey.
CHARLES. Yes sir?
VINNIE. Is "incidence" a word?

(Beat.)

CHARLES. Pardon me—?
VINNIE. Is "incidence" a word?
ANN-MARIE. You know, like in *"co*-incidence?"

(VINNIE shoots ANN-MARIE a look. CHARLES senses that he has walked into a domestic quarrel. He weighs his options carefully.)

CHARLES. I'm afraid I don't know, sir.
VINNIE. Yeah, well, you go *look*.
CHARLES. Sir?
VINNIE. You got a damn dictionary in this friggin' place?
CHARLES. I don't believe—
VINNIE. Hey! What I'm payin' for this suit? I coulda bought a car!
CHARLES. I don't think—
ANN-MARIE. *You* heard him! Go get a damn dictionary!!
CHARLES. Yes ma'am.

(CHARLES goes. Beat.)

VINNIE. *Now* we'll see.
ANN-MARIE. We sure will.

(Beat; VINNIE looks at himself in the mirror.)

VINNIE. It's not a word.
ANN-MARIE. "Incidence" is too a word.
VINNIE. No it's not; it's just a fragment of your imagination.
ANN-MARIE. You mean, frigment.
VINNIE. Hey. Did I say "frigment?" No. What'd I say?
ANN-MARIE. You said—
VINNIE. I said "fragment." Don't tell me what I did say and didn't say. Maybe we need to buy you a box a Q-Tips. You want me to go,

you want me to go over to that Pathmark downna block and buy you a box a Q-Tips? Clean your ears out so you can hear what I'm *sayin'* to you?

ANN-MARIE. No!

VINNIE. All right, then! *(Beat.)* You see now? Now you see. This is what I been talking about.

ANN-MARIE. What?

VINNIE. Why I don't wanna have kids.

ANN-MARIE. What?

VINNIE. This is just one of the reasons.

ANN-MARIE. What? This?

VINNIE. Yes.

ANN-MARIE. Us screamin' at each other in a Public Place?

VINNIE. Hey. This ain't a Public Place.

ANN-MARIE. I think it is, Wise Guy.

VINNIE. How many times do I have to tell you, don't call me that? And that ain't even the reason I'm talking about.

ANN-MARIE. What then?

VINNIE. Huh?

ANN-MARIE. What's the reason?

VINNIE. That you don't know no English.

ANN-MARIE. What?

VINNIE. That you can't practically speak no English!

ANN-MARIE. Well then what the hell's comin' outta my mouth, eh? Egyptian?

VINNIE. This is what I'm saying: That if we have a kid, he's gonna grow up with some kinda crap that can't nobody understand comin' outta his mouth alla time 'causa you and the way you talk!

ANN-MARIE. *(Shocked and hurt:)* That is a horrible thing ta say!

VINNIE. It's true!

ANN-MARIE. What makes you say a thing like that?

VINNIE. That guy.

ANN-MARIE. What guy?

VINNIE. At the Pizza place. He hadda ask you three times what the hell it was you wanted!

ANN-MARIE. It was *loud* in there!

VINNIE. You said—I heard ya!—you told him you wanted a large pie "with that red stuff on it!"

ANN-MARIE. So?

VINNIE. The word is "Pepperoni!"

ANN-MARIE. I *pointed* to it!

VINNIE. What good's raisin' a kid if he don't know common average words like "pepperoni?" *(CHARLES enters with the diction-*

ary. It is open and he has presumably found the word in question.)
Well?

CHARLES. "Incidence: An act or the fact or manner of falling upon or affecting."

ANN-MARIE. Hah!

VINNIE. Keep goin' ...

CHARLES. "The arrival of something ... "

ANN-MARIE. That's it!

VINNIE. No, it's not.

ANN-MARIE. It is *too*!

VINNIE. Lemme see that.

(VINNIE takes the dictionary.)

ANN-MARIE. He's such a spoil sport.

CHARLES. Shall I mark the bottoms, sir?

VINNIE. *(Lost in the book:)* Ah ... yeah. Go ahead.

(CHARLES kneels down, takes a box of pins, begins to arrange the cuffs and pin them.)

ANN-MARIE. What're you lookin' for now?

VINNIE. The *real* word you meant to say.

ANN-MARIE. I *said* what I meant to say. *You're* the one who needs the damn Q-Tips. Sore loser. *(She sticks her tongue out at VINNIE, then, to CHARLES:)* When you're done with the pants, go get him a box a Q-Tips!

VINNIE. "Incident."

ANN-MARIE. What?

VINNIE. That was what you *meant* to say.

ANN-MARIE. What?

VINNIE. You said "incidence" but you meant "incident."

ANN-MARIE. I said what I meant to say and you heard what I said and he proved what I said was okay to say!

(VINNIE bolts towards her with the book in hand, causing CHARLES to prick himself with the pin. He begins to bleed.)

CHARLES. Ah!

(VINNIE advances on her, rips a page out of the book, shoves it in her face and flings the rest of the book upstage. It lands with a loud "thud.")

VINNIE. Read this page! You got that? Read it and learn how to talk some English!

ANN-MARIE. I'll *tell* you what I'm gonna do! *(She goes to the dictionary and picks it up. CHARLES has moved to where VINNIE now stands and alternates between pinning the bottoms of the pants and sucking his bleeding thumb.)* I will read this damn book from cover to cover. Will that make you happy? I will learn every word *in* this whole dictionary and I will speak better English than anybody you ever *knew*! Will that make you satisfied? Huh? If I speak like the *Pope* whenever I open my mouth to talk, then maybe, *maybe*, can we talk about havin' a kid then?

(Pause. All, including CHARLES, wait for an answer. VINNIE considers this. Then,)

VINNIE. Yeah, okay. *(Beat.)* Maybe.

ANN-MARIE. *(Under her breath as she returns to her seat:)* I dunno why you're so scared a kids.

VINNIE. *(Who didn't catch this:)* What?

ANN-MARIE. Nothin'!

(ANN-MARIE sits and begins reading the dictionary from page one.)

CHARLES. Would you like cuffs or no cuffs, sir?

VINNIE. *(Sneering:) No* cuffs. What, you want me to look like a *businessman*? And gimme a little more break in the leg. *(CHARLES obeys.)* Yeah. Good. That's good. And—hey! Don't bleed all over the pants, willya? For cryin' out loud! What I'm *payin'* for these?

ANN-MARIE. Wow.

VINNIE. What?

ANN-MARIE. Aardvark's in here.

VINNIE. Are what?

ANN-MARIE. I though an aardvark was just a cartoon character.

VINNIE. What the hell are you talkin' about?

ANN-MARIE. You know, "The Ant and the Aardvark?"

VINNIE. Jeez. You didn't learn *nothin'* in that damn Catholic School, did ya? Just how ta hike up your skirt.

ANN-MARIE. *That's* a horrible thing to say!

VINNIE. It's true!

ANN-MARIE. In front of a stranger?

VINNIE. Charles ain't a stranger, he tailors alla my clothes.

CHARLES. I can assure you Madam, I am not listening to this

conversation.

ANN-MARIE. "A large burrowing nocturnal African mammal."
Hmm. What's "nocturnal" mean?

VINNIE. It means stupid.

(VINNIE laughs at his joke.)

CHARLES. How's the jacket, sir?

VINNIE. Eh? Oh, good. It's fine just like it is.

CHARLES. Very well, sir.

*(VINNIE takes it off, hands it to CHARLES. We now see that VINNIE
wears a shoulder holster.)*

ANN-MARIE. "Nocturnal. Active at night."

VINNIE. *(Uninterested:)* Well whaddya know.

ANN-MARIE. "Nocturne ... a work of art dealing with night."
Sounds kinda like you, Vinnie.

VINNIE. Yeah?

ANN-MARIE. Yeah. *(He smiles, goes to her, kisses her. A warm
moment.)* I'm gonna read this whole entire book, Vinnie.

VINNIE. That's nice, babe. You been needin' a hobby.

*(VINNIE takes off the pants, hands them to CHARLES, puts his own
on.)*

ANN-MARIE. *Then* can we talk about havin' kids?

VINNIE. You just finish readin' that book, honey. You finish that
book and we can talk about kids all you want.

CHARLES. Will there be anything else, sir?

VINNIE. Nah. 'At's all.

*(VINNIE takes out a huge wad of bills, peels several off and hands
them to CHARLES.)*

CHARLES. Thank you, sir.

VINNIE. Oh. And I need the suit by noon Friday.

CHARLES. Yes sir.

VINNIE. It has to be ready on Friday.

CHARLES. All right.

VINNIE. This is very important.

(CHARLES nods, gathers up the suit.)

ANN-MARIE. *(Regarding VINNIE fondly:)* Friday's a big night
for Vinnie.

VINNIE. Friday ... is the biggest night a my life, babe.

*(VINNIE and ANN-MARIE gaze at each other, sharing something
   profound.)*
(Blackout.)

Scene 2

(SETTING: Late Thursday afternoon.
AT RISE: VINNIE and ANN-MARIE in VINNIE's car. VINNIE drives.
   He is now attired in his "regular" duds, a leather sportcoat and
   an appropriate number of gold chains. ANN-MARIE reads her
   dictionary as they drive. Silence for a moment, then:)

VINNIE. Nice neighborhood, eh?

ANN-MARIE. *(Looking up:)* Yeah, real nice. Lookit them pretty
Christmas lights ...

VINNIE. They keep 'em up all year round.

ANN-MARIE. That's nice. *(Beat; they look.)* Think we'll get ta
move here now?

VINNIE. I dunno. Maybe. Probably. Eventually ... *(ANN-MARIE
goes back to her book.)* These guys are all doin' mighty well for
themselves, I'm tellin' you. Lookit them satellite dishes! Every house
on this block's got a sat— *(VINNIE sees that she is not paying attention.)* Hey! I am trying to show you something here!

ANN-MARIE. What?

VINNIE. Look!

ANN-MARIE. Satellite dishes? *(He nods.)* I *seen* satellite dishes
before!

VINNIE. But lookit these *houses*!

ANN-MARIE. *(She does, and she's impressed:)* Mmmmm ...
they're nice.

VINNIE. I'm tellin' ya. And, the coup de grass—

ANN-MARIE. The *what*?

VINNIE. Coup de grass. You know, The, the crownin' touch—
(She consults her dictionary.) Oh, c'mon now! Enough with this!
You gotta look up every word that comes outta my *mouth*?

ANN-MARIE. I'm jus' checkin' ...

VINNIE. Well do me a favor: *don't*. All right?

ANN-MARIE. *(Closing the book again:)* All right! Jeez, make up your mind why doncha. First you want me to read the book, then you don't want me to ...

VINNIE. What I *wanted* was for you to learn how to talk like a human bean!

ANN-MARIE. I'm *tryin'*!

VINNIE. Well, not *now*!

ANN-MARIE. Why not?

VINNIE. Because! I'm trying to *show* you! *(Beat; she drums her long polished nails on the cover of the dictionary. This really irritates him. Silence for a moment. Then, an oft-repeated rule:)* No clickin' in the car.

(She stops, fumes silently. They drive on.)

ANN-MARIE. Okay, look. You just tell me. All right? Tell me what the hell it is you want from me and I'll do it. Okay?

VINNIE. Okay.

ANN-MARIE. Okay?

VINNIE. OKAY! LOOKIT THE HOUSES!

(She glances in front of them, stomps her feet as if stepping on imaginary brakes, reacts to something in the road before them:)

ANN-MARIE. VINNIE!

VINNIE. What—?

ANN-MARIE. —LOOK OUT FOR THAT KID—!!

VINNIE. Oh my God—!

(VINNIE swerves.)

ANN-MARIE. —THAT LITTLE BOY!

VINNIE. —I KNOW, I SAW HIM—!

ANN-MARIE. YOU ALMOST HIT THAT—

VINNIE. —I DID *NOT*!

ANN-MARIE. He came this close—

VINNIE. He shouldn't a been playin'—

ANN-MARIE. —this close to the—

VINNIE. —out in the—*(Out the window:)* Hey, kid! Watch it, willya? *(Beat.)* Yeah, well don't *throw* it out in the middle a the street next time! *(VINNIE looks closer at the unseen "kid," pales. NOTE: We never see the kid in this scene.)* Oh, my God ...

ANN-MARIE. What?

VINNIE. You know who that *is*?

ANN-MARIE. Who?

VINNIE. That kid.

ANN-MARIE. Who?

VINNIE. It's Tommy.

ANN-MARIE. Who?

VINNIE. Little Tommy Roselli.

ANN-MARIE. Oh ...

VINNIE. The Boss's kid!

ANN-MARIE. Really?

VINNIE. *(Trying to look closer:)* I, I think so ...

ANN-MARIE. He's gettin' big.

VINNIE. Yeah, he's like, six now I think.

ANN-MARIE. Wow ...

VINNIE. Oh my God! I just yelled at the Boss's kid!

ANN-MARIE. You almost just ran *over* the Boss's kid!

VINNIE. Oh my God ...

ANN-MARIE. Don't worry about it.

VINNIE. You don't yell at the Boss's kid.

ANN-MARIE. He was in the middle a the street!

VINNIE. When he was in Nursery School, his teacher yelled at him for getting fingerpaints all in her hair.

ANN-MARIE. For—?

VINNIE. Yeah.

ANN-MARIE. Aw ... Idn't that cute?

VINNIE. Cute? It's a pain in the ass! Would you want fingerpaints in your hair?

ANN-MARIE. So what happened?

VINNIE. She yelled at him! Yeah! She tells him next time he gets fingerpaints in her hair she's gonna smack the crap outta him.

ANN-MARIE. So?

VINNIE. *So* ... the Boss sends Joey "the Mole" D'Angella and Bobby "Thumbnails" Squizeri over to that school to pay her a little visit.

ANN-MARIE. Who, the teacher?

VINNIE. Yeah.

ANN-MARIE. And?

VINNIE. Well ... I ain't at liberty to talk descriptionally, but just lemme say, that woman's teachin' from a *wheelchair* nowdays.

ANN-MARIE. My God!

VINNIE. I'm tellin' ya, babe. You don't mess around with the Boss or his offstring. This guy— *(He stops the car, looks up in awe.)*

—ooh, there it is. The Boss's Home.

ANN-MARIE. *(Overwhelmed:)* Wow.

VINNIE. Idn't it somethin'?

ANN-MARIE. It looks like a castle!

VINNIE. S'gotta be. To protect a guy like *him*? Fuggettaboutit.

ANN-MARIE. Wow.

VINNIE. Here, lemme turn around. *(He does so as ANN-MARIE gazes worshipfully at the "castle.")* That's where it's all gonna happen, honey. See that basement window? *(She nods.)* Tomorra night. I'm goin' in there Vinnie Rampulo ... but I'm comin' out a Made Man.

ANN-MARIE. *(Her eyes brimming with tears:)* Vinnie! I'm so proud a you!

VINNIE. *(Shrugging it off:)* Ah ...

ANN-MARIE. I can't wait 'till we have a house like this one day.

VINNIE. Be nice, won't it?

ANN-MARIE. First thing I'm gonna do, I'm gonna have me a party. And I'm gonna invite over alla them girls I grew up with. Rosa Vincentelli ... Bella DeRazio ... she thinks she's so hot 'cause she married some Jewish doctor. And that gimp Rosa married owns a few lousy restaurants—but I'll show *them*! All my life, alla time growin' up they both treated me like dirt cause we didn't have nothin' and they both did. But you just wait. One day we'll have a house like this and a car like that and I'll rub their noses in it! Drive by their houses three times a day in my Cadillac and honk the horn!

VINNIE. Ann-Marie—

ANN-MARIE. "Your husband's a doctor but you're still a pig!"

VINNIE. Easy, easy now.

ANN-MARIE. Oh. Oh ...

VINNIE. You're gettin' carried away again.

ANN-MARIE. I'm sorry. I just—

VINNIE. I mean, greed is good, you know, but only in medium-sized does.

Ann-MARIE. Yeah.

VINNIE. Listen. Don't you worry. We'll show 'em.

ANN-MARIE. I know.

VINNIE. We'll show 'em *all*.

ANN-MARIE. Yeah.

VINNIE. Just stick with me, baby.

ANN-MARIE. I will.

VINNIE. Stick with me and we'll be sittin' in that castle one day!

(She laughs. He joins her.)

ANN-MARIE. Yeah, well. I'm still gonna call her up.

VINNIE. Who?

ANN-MARIE. Bella. Bella Rosenbaum, s'her name now. I'm gonna tell her all about you.

VINNIE. Ann-Marie! No!

ANN-MARIE. I want to!

VINNIE. You can't!

ANN-MARIE. But I'm *proud* a you!

VINNIE. I know, I am too, but you can't go trumpetin' this around to alla your friends!

ANN-MARIE. She is *not* my friend.

VINNIE. You still can't be callin' her up and talkin' about this!

ANN-MARIE. Why not?

VINNIE. Because! This is sacred, Ann-Marie! This is a sacred secret, I'm not even s'posed to be tellin' you!

ANN-MARIE. Sacred?

VINNIE. Yes! *(ANN-MARIE consults her book.)* What?

ANN-MARIE. ... I just wanna *see* ...

VINNIE. You're not gonna look it *up*!

ANN-MARIE. I just wanna see!

VINNIE. Every fifth word outta my mouth!

ANN-MARIE. *(Looking for it.)* Sacred, sacred, sacred ...

VINNIE. Ann-Marie!

ANN-MARIE. *(Glancing up quickly:)* Look. There's somebody in the window.

VINNIE. Crap!

(VINNIE puts the car in drive, starts to go.)

ANN-MARIE. *(Looking again:)* I just wanted ta see ...

VINNIE. Put that damn book away, you hear me?

ANN-MARIE. "Sacred. To set apart for the service of worship or deity."

VINNIE. Ann-Marie!

ANN-MARIE. "Worthy of religious veneration ... "

VINNIE. Give it to me!

ANN-MARIE. " ... entitled to reverence ... "

VINNIE. NOW!

(VINNIE lunges for the book. ANN-MARIE looks up, sees something in front of them.)

ANN-MARIE. VINNIE! LOOK OUT!!!

(VINNIE looks up and his eyes widen in terror. He hits the brakes. We hear a squeal of brakes and he tries to swerve. Sound of a loud "thump." Silence. VINNIE and ANN-MARIE sit for a moment, then turn and look at each other.)

VINNIE. Was that—?
ANN-MARIE. I think so.
VINNIE. Oh my God ...
ANN-MARIE. Vinnie.
VINNIE. No.
ANN-MARIE. Vinnie!
VINNIE. It can't be!
ANN-MARIE. You just hit the Boss's *kid*! *(Beat.)* What do we do now? Call an ambulance or somethin'?
VINNIE. Did anybody see?
ANN-MARIE. What?
VINNIE. Did anybody *see*?

(Beat; they both look around.)

ANN-MARIE. I don't think so ...
VINNIE. Good. Get outta the car.
ANN-MARIE. What?
VINNIE. Get outta the car and get the kid.
ANN-MARIE. What?
VINNIE. Get him!
ANN-MARIE. What am I supposed to do with him?
VINNIE. Put him in the back seat.
ANN-MARIE. Maybe he's hurt! Maybe we shouldn't be movin' him!
VINNIE. Do what I tell ya! Get outta the car and get the kid now!
ANN-MARIE. And just what the hell are you gonna *do* with him?

(Beat.)

VINNIE. I dunno ...
ANN-MARIE. Vinnie!
VINNIE. Get him! Now! Or we're both gonna wind up split into a million different pieces, fillin' up nine suitcases in the Port Authority Bus Terminal!

(ANN-MARIE starts to move.)

(Blackout.)

Scene 3

(SETTING: Thursday evening. VINNIE and ANN-MARIE's bedroom.)
(AT RISE: The KID is out cold on the bed. ANN-MARIE pouts in
front of her vanity. VINNIE hovers over the KID, looking for signs
of life. A long pause. Then:)

ANN-MARIE. I hate you.
VINNIE. Ann-Marie, I'm sorry ...
ANN-MARIE. I can't *believe* you made me *do* that!
VINNIE. Ann-Marie—
ANN-MARIE. Made me *humilerate* myself like that!
VINNIE. I said I'm sorry!
ANN-MARIE. You made me get down on my knees ...
VINNIE. Ann-Marie—
ANN-MARIE. ... call *Bella Rosenbaum* ...
VINNIE. Listen to me—
ANN-MARIE. ... and ask her for a FAVOR!!!!

(Beat. VINNIE tries to reason.)

VINNIE. Ann-Marie. We had no choice.
ANN-MARIE. I HATE YOU!
VINNIE. What'd you expect me to do, eh? Drive back to the Boss's house and ring the doorbell? Ding-dong. "Hey, Boss, we just ran over your *kid!*"
ANN-MARIE. My skin feels like it is just crawling with ants.
VINNIE. So? You can go to the spa tomorrow. You'll be fine.
ANN-MARIE. That won't make this feelin' go away. This is an *inside-a-me* feelin'. It comes from bein' subtracted to total humilerating behavior! God, I feel like I just ast somebody for *money* or somethin'!
VINNIE. Look. You didn't ask her for the favor, okay? You asked her *husband.*
ANN-MARIE. It's the same thing!
VINNIE. It is *not* the same thing! If I get told to whack some guy out, that's *me* doin' it, not you!
ANN-MARIE. But *you* weren't the one, hadda beg a favor from Bella Rosenbaum—

VINNIE. FOR THE LAST TIME—   .

(Doorbell rings.)

ANN-MARIE. There he is! I hope to God he didn't bring *her* along with him!

VINNIE. Let 'em in.

ANN-MARIE. I will *die* if she's with him. Lookit this house. It looks like a hellhole!

VINNIE. It looks fine, now let him in!

ANN-MARIE. You!

VINNIE. Ann-Marie—

ANN-MARIE. *You* ran over the kid! You get it! Besides, you oughtta be on your hands and knees thankin' me right now, kissin' my feet cause I know somebody whose husband is a *doctor* or you'd be up shit's lake right now!

(The doorbell again.)

VINNIE. Okay. Fine. I'll get the door. But you *watch* him!

(VINNIE goes. ANN-MARIE goes to the child, puts a damp cloth on his forehead, suddenly transforming into a very loving woman.)

ANN-MARIE. Shhhh ... S'okay, honey. S'all gonna be okay ...
(VINNIE leads DR. ROSENBAUM in.) Doctor! Thank you for comin'.

ROSENBAUM. I was happy to. Bella said to say hi, she couldn't come with me.

ANN-MARIE. Thank God.

ROSENBAUM. What?

ANN-MARIE. Thank God *you* could come!

VINNIE. Here he is, Doctor.

(DR. ROSENBAUM moves in closer, looks at the boy.)

ROSENBAUM. Bella was surprised, she didn't know you had children.

ANN-MARIE. Just the one.

VINNIE. Just him. He's our boy.

ROSENBAUM. Mm-hmm. What's his name?

VINNIE.   ANN-MARIE.
Billy.   Joey.

(Beat. ANN-MARIE swallows her pride and tries to maintain dignity as well as the lie:)

ANN-MARIE. Billy ... Joe.

ROSENBAUM. Okay. So ... what exactly happened?

ANN-MARIE. *(With great verve.)* He was playin' out front. In the street. Vinnie's done told him about 150 times about *not* playin' in the street, but does he listen?

VINNIE. Ann-Marie—

ANN-MARIE. *(Really on a roll now:)* No! He don't listen! I was in the kitchen knitting ... *things* for him ta wear when all of a sudden I hear this screech of tires and this "whump!" And I run outside to find little Billy Joe lyin' face down in the street and a car speedin' away.

ROSENBAUM. Did you get a good look at the car?

ANN-MARIE. Ah ... no.

VINNIE. Actually, she just *heard* the car.

ANN-MARIE. Yeah. I heard the car, speeding away.

ROSENBAUM. That's a pretty busy street out there, you really should try to keep an eye on him.

ANN-MARIE. I was busy! Whaddya *want from me*?

VINNIE. Ah ... listen, doc. Is he gonna be okay?

ROSENBAUM. Well ...

VINNIE. Please say he's gonna be okay.

ROSENBAUM. Like I tried to tell you on the phone. I'm a Podiatrist.

VINNIE. We don't care about your religious beliefs.

ROSENBAUM. *(He laughs, actually thinking VINNIE is making a joke.)* I mean, I studied General Medicine at B.U. and I probably can help you. But I don't understand why you just didn't take him to a hospital.

VINNIE I, ah, I once had a very, very bad experience at a hospital. One time.

ROSENBAUM. I'm so sorry to hear that.

ANN-MARIE. *(Who has finally found what she's looking for:)* A FOOT DOCTOR?

(She looks accusingly at the DOCTOR.)

ROSENBAUM. Well ... yes.

VINNIE. What?

ANN-MARIE. Bella married a Jewish Foot Doctor?

ROSENBAUM. I—

ANN-MARIE. Hah! And here I was, this whole time, thinkin' she married herself a *real* doctor!

ROSENBAUM. I *am* a real doctor!

ANN-MARIE. The kid don't have hammertoes, Doc!

ROSENBAUM. I know! I can see that!

ANN-MARIE. So what the hell you gonna do?

VINNIE. Ann-Marie—

ANN-MARIE. —what's he gonna do? Huh? Check to see if he's got *bunions*?

ROSENBAUM. *(To prove his competence.)* The boy is obviously in shock.

ANN-MARIE. Oh, like we didn't already know that?

ROSENBAUM ... and it looks like a compound fracture on the left arm.

ANN-MARIE. Uh-huh ...

VINNIE. So that's all it is, Doc? A broken arm?

ROSENBAUM. I don't know for certain. You say he was hit by a *car*?

ANN-MARIE. That's what we done *told* you! *(To VINNIE:)* Get *him* the Q-Tips, why doncha.

VINNIE. Yes, Doctor.

ROSENBAUM. I'd want x-rays, if I were you. There could be internal hemorrhaging ... contusions ... you can't tell just from *looking* at him.

ANN-MARIE. Oh, but his *toenails* look a-okay, eh, Doc?

ROSENBAUM. *(Trying to stay calm:)* I have a friend who's an internist in New Jersey. I understand that you have some, some resistance to hospitals and so forth, but the boy really needs x-rays. If you want to take the boy out there, I could call ahead and tell Dr. McCaffrey that you're coming.

VINNIE. Yeah. That's a good idea. Call up and say we're coming.

(VINNIE points to the phone; ROSENBAUM goes to it and begins dialing.)

ROSENBAUM. What's your insurance company?

(Beat. ANN-MARIE and VINNIE look at each other, shrug.)

VINNIE. Insurance?

ROSENBAUM. Yes. *(Into phone:)* Dr. McCaffrey, please.

VINNIE. We don't got none.

ROSENBAUM. You don't—? *(Into phone:)* Thank you.

VINNIE. We always just pay cash for everything.

(Beat.)

ROSENBAUM. Well, I'll let you sort that out with the—Hello? Dr. McCaffrey? Fred Rosenbaum here. Listen. I have some, some friends with me who could use your help ...

(VINNIE looks at ANN-MARIE. Blackout.)

Scene 4

(SETTING: Later Thursday night. Hospital examining room.
AT RISE: The KID is still out cold, though now laid on an examining table. VINNIE and ANN-MARIE wait nervously for the DOCTOR.)

VINNIE. He still out?
ANN-MARIE. What's it *look* like?
VINNIE. He's not dead, is he?
ANN-MARIE. How the hell should I know? *You're* the one's so used to seein' stiffs.
VINNIE. Ha, ha. You're just a regular Donna Rickles, ain't ya?
ANN-MARIE. He's still breathin', if that's whatcha mean.

(Beat.)

VINNIE. I wisht he'd *say* somethin'!
ANN-MARIE. Like what?
VINNIE. I dunno. Anything. So we'd know he's okay.

(Beat; they watch the boy. As ANN-MARIE gazes at the lad, she visually softens.)

ANN-MARIE. Idn't he sweet?
VINNIE. Who, the doctor?
ANN-MARIE. No, stupid! The kid! Look. Isn't he cute?
VINNIE. They're always cute when they're sleepin'.
ANN-MARIE. But look at him. *(VINNIE does.)* Don't it make you want one?
VINNIE. No.
ANN-MARIE. Just a little?

VINNIE. I hear that biographical clock a yours tickin' and I wisht I could cut it off!

ANN-MARIE. But he's so adorable.

VINNIE. He ran out in front of our car, Ann-Marie.

ANN-MARIE. Well, you were barrellin' down the middle of the road like some kinda maniac!

VINNIE. Okay, okay, look. Enough. Can we just stop?

ANN-MARIE. Stop what?

VINNIE. Fightin' like cats and birds?

ANN-MARIE. *You* started it!

VINNIE. I'm sorry then. Okay?

ANN-MARIE. Okay.

VINNIE. Truce?

(ANN-MARIE looks at VINNIE a moment, then reaches for her dictionary.)

VINNIE. I can't believe it! You brought that damn *book* in here?

ANN-MARIE. I hadda have it! Just in case they start throwin' around fancy medical terms, I wanna know what they're sayin'!

VINNIE. Look. Before you adopt this kid and build an extra room onto our house, lemme just *tell* you.

ANN-MARIE. Tell me what?

VINNIE. As soon as they fix his arm or whatever it is that's wrong with him, that's it.

ANN-MARIE. What?

VINNIE. Your little stint as Mother Teresa is over!

ANN-MARIE. Whaddya mean?

VINNIE. I *mean* he's gotta go back home!

ANN-MARIE. No!

VINNIE. What the hell did you *think*? Huh?

ANN-MARIE. But I wanted to take care of him! Nurse him back to health! Couldn't we just keep him for a little while?

VINNIE. No!

ANN-MARIE. Why not?

VINNIE. Because! He's not *ours*! How many times I hafta tell you that?

ANN-MARIE. But I want one!

VINNIE. Not him!

ANN-MARIE. Please?

VINNIE. Look. We are takin' him back to his neighborhood tonight and we are stashin' him in the bushes someplace.

ANN-MARIE. Like some ol' stray cat?

VINNIE. Hopefully he'll wake up and find his way home and nobody'll know *what* the hell happened.

ANN-MARIE. Like some ol' stray cat!

VINNIE. Stop it! All right? Look. Take a good, long look at this kid. Look at him! One a these days, he is gonna grow up to be the Don! He's gonna snap his fingers and people's gonna die! He's gonna be the most evil guy in the whole damn borough!

ANN-MARIE. He's not evil *now.*

VINNIE. He will be, don't you worry.

ANN-MARIE. That's only if you *teach* him ta be.

VINNIE. Well, his dad is the best teacher around, lemme tell you.

ANN-MARIE. So then that's *another* reason we should keep him!

VINNIE. *(Who cannot believe his ears:)* What?

ANN-MARIE. So we can raise him up to be nice little boy. He could grow up to run a, a hobby shop or somethin'. Sell little electric trains and little plastic people ...

VINNIE. Ann-Marie! This kid is goin' home where he belongs! And if you don't shut your trap, I'm gonna knock the crap outta you myself!

(VINNIE raises a threatening hand to her—not really to hit her, but just to make his point. Unfortunately, DR. McCAFFREY has entered on the last bit of this line and she is, very understandably, quite surprised.)

McCAFFREY. Oh.
VINNIE. Whadyou want?
McCAFFREY. I'm Dr. McCaffrey.

(Beat.)

ANN- MARIE. Come on in!

McCAFFREY. *(Taking an instant dislike to VINNIE:)* I seem to have walked into the middle of a—

ANN-MARIE. Thank you for—

McCAFFREY. —a domestic quarrel or something.

VINNIE. That wadn't no quarrel, lady. That wadn't nothin' at all. You know how it is, sometimes you just hafta knock 'em around a little.

(VINNIE chuckles at his joke. No one else does. An uncomfortable pause. Then:)

McCAFFREY. So ... this is Billy Joe?
ANN-MARIE. Yes, Doctor.

McCAFFREY. *(Examining the boy:)* I understand it's something with his arm ...

ANN-MARIE. Yes ma'am.

VINNIE. Lemme ask you something. Are you a *real* doctor?

(Beat.)

McCAFFREY. Yes. *(VINNIE nods. McCAFFREY turns back to the boy.)* How long ago did this happen?

ANN-MARIE. I dunno, around—

(She looks to VINNIE for help.)

VINNIE. Coupla hours ago.

McCAFFREY. And he's been unconscious the whole *time*?

ANN-MARIE. Yes ma'am.

(McCAFFREY gets some ammonia capsules.)

McCAFFREY. Why didn't you call an ambulance?

ANN-MARIE. Well, we—

VINNIE. Lemme handle this, Ann-Marie. *(VINNIE steps forward.)* We thought he was okay. Now you gonna give us the third degree here or fix his arm?

McCAFFREY. "Fix his arm?" Will you take a good long look? He's got a bone protrusion that a blind man could see! What are you, some kind of Neanderthal?

(ANN-MARIE gets the dictionary.)

VINNIE. Hey! Don't mess with me, lady. You go that? *(To ANN-MARIE:)* And you! Put that damn book down before I knock you in the head with it!

ANN-MARIE. I'm lookin' up Meanderthal.

McCAFFREY. *Ne*-anderthal.

VINNIE. It means caveman.

McCAFFREY. Let's see if we can get him to come around.

VINNIE. Oh, hey. You sure you wanna do that, Doc?

McCAFFREY. I want to make sure he's alert. That there's no damage to the brain.

VINNIE. He got hit in the *arm*, not his *head*! Did you pass medical school, or what?

McCAFFREY. I have to make sure.

VINNIE. Maybe you could give him some x-rays or somethin'.
McCAFFREY. I *will*, but first I am going to—Look! Do you *mind*
if I do my job?
VINNIE. Excuse me for livin'!
McCAFFREY. Is that okay with you?
VINNIE. Okay!

(DR. McCAFFREY breaks an ammonia capsule, waves it under the
boy's nose. The boy stirs. VINNIE and ANN-MARIE tense in ex-
pectation.)

McCAFFREY. Shhh, shhh. It's okay ...

(VINNIE, frozen in terror, backs away from the child. ANN-MARIE
jumps in, playing the role of caring mother.)

ANN-MARIE. Honey? Honey? It's Mommy ...
McCAFFREY. Son? Can you hear me?

(The boy opens his eyes, frightened.)

KID. Where, where am I—?
McCAFFREY. Shhh. You had an accident. But everything's okay.
KID. My arm!
McCAFFREY. I know. I know, we're gonna take good care of
you now.

(A beeper goes off. Both VINNIE and McCAFFREY check to see if
it's them. It's VINNIE.)

VINNIE. It's me. Is there a phone here someplace?
McCAFFREY. There's a pay phone in the hall.
VINNIE. I'll be right back.

(VINNIE goes. The KID is stirring now.)

KID. Daddy!
ANN-MARIE. Daddy just went to make a phone call, baby.
McCAFFREY. Shhh. It's okay ...
KID. Where's Mommy?
ANN-MARIE. I'm ... right here, sweetheart.
KID. You're not my Mommy!
ANN-MARIE. Shhhh.

KID. Where's my Mommy?

McCAFFREY. Shhh. Just lie back, now.

ANN-MARIE. He's dysterical, Doctor.

McCAFFREY. I know, he's frightened of *something*—

KID. DADDY!

ANN-MARIE. He'll be back in a minute, honey.

KID. *(Crying now:)* DADDY!!!

ANN-MARIE. Help me—! He's moving!

McCAFFREY. I'm going to put him under.

ANN-MARIE. That's good.

McCAFFREY. So we can—it's okay, honey—set his arm.

ANN-MARIE. Good idea.

KID. You're hurting me! Daddy!

(VINNIE re-enters.)

ANN-MARIE. Here's Daddy, honey.

KID. He's not my Daddy!

McCAFFREY. Shhhh.

VINNIE. Hey! What's wrong ... sport?

KID. He yelled at me!

VINNIE. Son.

KID. Get away from me! Daddy!

McCAFFREY. Billy Joe—

KID. That's not my name! That's not my name! I WANT MY DADDY!!!

VINNIE. Doc, he's, he's talking nonsense!

McCAFFREY. Son, this is going to hurt just a little.

KID. NO!!

McCAFFREY. Hold him.

(ANN-MARIE obeys. McCAFFREY gives the KID a shot.)

KID. *(Wailing now:)* HELP ME!!! HELP ME!!!

McCAFFREY. Shhh. It's okay. Lie back now.

KID. DADDY!

McCAFFREY. Shhhh. Shhh ...

(McCAFFREY strokes the boy's hair, "shhing" him to still him. He calms very quickly, becomes quiet. She continues stroking his hair. He begins to drift off. It is quiet now.)

VINNIE. Ahem. I, ah ... I gotta go.

(McCAFFREY shoots him a look.)

    ANN-MARIE. Go?
    VINNIE. That was the *Boss.*
    ANN-MARIE. Oh.
    VINNIE. On the phone.
    ANN-MARIE. Oh.
    VINNIE. Yeah.

(Beat.)

    ANN-MARIE. Well ...
    VINNIE. Look. Stay with the kid, okay?
    ANN-MARIE. Okay.

(Beat; VINNIE senses that his "role" as father hangs in doubt. The DOCTOR is scrutinizing his every move. VINNIE strolls over to the boy and awkwardly pats his prostrate form.)

    VINNIE. Take it easy ... wise guy.

(The act is, needless to say, not very convincing—not very paternal I should say. VINNIE goes. McCAFFREY and ANN-MARIE watch him leave. The DOCTOR turns and looks at ANN-MARIE. Pause ANN-MARIE shrugs.)

    ANN-MARIE. You got a bathroom in here someplace?

(Blackout.)

Scene 5

(SETTING: A bit later. The BOSS's house.
AT RISE: The BOSS sits alone in a leather recliner chair in his base-ment. The room is very dark, you can barely see the BOSS in the shadows. Perhaps there are more people in the room, you can't tell. Which adds to VINNIE's trepidation as he enters and stands there in the dark for a long, long time. Finally:)

    VINNIE. Boss?

(Beat.)

BOSS. Vinnie?
VINNIE. Yeah.
BOSS. S'that you, Vinnie?
VINNIE. Ah ... yeah.
BOSS. Have a seat.

(VINNIE attempts to, stumbles on something in the dark, finally finds a seat. Pause.)

VINNIE. What's a matter, Boss?
BOSS. A matter?
VINNIE. Well, you're sittin' down here in the dark.
BOSS. Is it dark down here?
VINNIE. Well ... yeah.
BOSS. I lost track of light and dark. Of time ... *(Beat.)* What time is it, Vinnie?
VINNIE. *(Has to really squint to see his watch:)* Ah ... *(It takes awhile.)* Can you turn on a—? Never mind, I got it. It's ... ah ... around nine, I guess.

(Long pause.)

BOSS. You ever notice how fast time moves, Vinnie?
VINNIE. Time?
BOSS. Mm-hmm.
VINNIE. I dunno. Yeah. Sure.
BOSS. The minutes run into hours ... the hours run into days ... the days run into weeks ... weeks into years ... and then you know what?
VINNIE. What? Into centuries or somethin'?
BOSS. No. Then we're dead.
VINNIE. Oh.
BOSS. Life is over. Ffft. Snuffed out, like a candle. Or, or a light bulb. You know when a light bulb burns out?
VINNIE. Yeah.
BOSS. One day, it's all over.

(Beat.)

VINNIE. So ... what's a matter, Boss? You're not, you're not dyin' or anything, are ya?

BOSS. We're all dying, Vinnie.

VINNIE. Oh.

BOSS. Slow-ly ...

VINNIE. Huh.

BOSS. We wake up one day and we're standing at death's door! And before we know it, we're ringin' the doorbell!

VINNIE. God!

BOSS. And when he opens that door ... well. That's it, Vinnie. It's all over. The light bulb is out.

VINNIE. Yeah.

(Beat.)

BOSS. And what do we have to show for our time on earth, Vinnie?

VINNIE. I dunno.

BOSS. Children.

VINNIE. Oh.

BOSS. All we have ... in the end ... is our children.

VINNIE. Uh-huh ...

VINNIE. Do you have any children, Vinnie?

VINNIE. Ah ... no, Boss. No, I don't.

BOSS. Then you don't know.

VINNIE. Know?

BOSS. The agony. Of waiting ... wondering ... hoping ...

VINNIE. What, what are you waiting and wondering about, Boss?

(The BOSS turns on a lamp beside his chair. It illuminates his face eerily from beneath.)

BOSS. You ever met my boy Tommy?

VINNIE. Ah ... yeah, I, I think so.

BOSS. Tommy's gonna be seven next July, Vinnie.

VINNIE. Wow.

BOSS. S'a good boy.

VINNIE. I know.

BOSS. You do?

VINNIE. You done told me.

BOSS. Mmm ... my boy, Tommy. He is my *life*, Vinnie. I ever tell you that?

VINNIE. Ah ... no.

BOSS. It's true. All my *money* ... all my status ... all my power ... the hell with all that. That means nothin'!

VINNIE. Hmmm.

BOSS. *Blood* is what matters. That special bond between a father and his son.

(Beat.)

VINNIE. Why ... why are you tellin' me all this, Boss?
BOSS. Why am I telling you all this?
VINNIE. Yeah. *(Silence.)* Where is everybody?
BOSS. Everybody?
VINNIE. You know. The *guys.*
BOSS. They're out looking.
VINNIE. Looking?
BOSS. For my boy, Tommy
VINNIE. Your—?
BOSS. He's missing.
VINNIE. No!
BOSS. Yes.
VINNIE. What happened?
BOSS. I don't know. Nobody knows. He just never came home for dinner.
VINNIE. Huh.
BOSS. Francesca fixed his favorite, too. Steak tartar.
VINNIE. Huh ...
BOSS. I think something's happened to him. Somebody's kidnapped him or—I dunno, *done* somethin' horrible to him! It's not like him not to come home. Why would a six-year-old not come home, Vinnie? Eh?
VINNIE. I dunno.
BOSS. Unless ... something's happened to him! You see? You see how it tortures a parent?
VINNIE. Yeah ...
BOSS. I got all the guys out lookin' for him. I want you to look, too.
VINNIE. Sure thing, Boss. Whatever you say.
BOSS. I'm gonna give 50,000 bucks to whoever finds my boy.
VINNIE. Fif—? Wow.
BOSS. Money is no object.
VINNIE. Uh-huh ...
BOSS. But I'm tellin' you ... if there's anything shady—what I mean by that—if anybody's *done* anything to my boy Tommy ...
VINNIE. Yeah?
BOSS. He's gonna wish he'd never been *born.*
VINNIE. Huh.

BOSS. *(Casually:)* You ever cut off a man's nuts, Vinnie?

VINNIE. Ah, no, I can't, I can't say that I have.

BOSS. What you hafta *do*, Vinnie, what you hafta do is watch his *face*.

VINNIE. Huh.

BOSS. *While* you're slicing his balls off.

VINNIE. Oooh.

BOSS. His face contorts into the most fascinating mask of pain, confusion, terror ... and ultimately, shame.

VINNIE. Sh—shame?

BOSS. Because he is no longer a *man,* Vinnie.

VINNIE. Oh.

BOSS. And he knows it. While you're cutting, while you're slicing—he knows, *if* he survives, that he will never be a *man* again.

VINNIE. What if ... let's just say ... what if it was a *woman*, Boss?

BOSS. A woman?

VINNIE. Yeah.

BOSS. A woman?

VINNIE. Well, you never know.

BOSS. Well, we'd figure out something equally painful for her.

VINNIE. Huh.

BOSS. Now get goin', Vinnie. Scour this neighborhood, this whole borough. Knock on every window, break down every door—

VINNIE. Yes sir!

BOSS. —but you find my boy and you bring my kid back to me!

VINNIE. Yes sir!

(VINNIE is about to go. GIUSEPPE, the BOSS's houseboy, enters. He goes to the BOSS and whispers in his ear in Italian. The BOSS looks at VINNIE. Pause.)

BOSS. You speak Italian, Vinnie?

VINNIE. I ... I used to. Back in the old neighborhood. I'm a little rusty now.

BOSS. This is Giuseppe. My houseboy. I brought him over from Sicily to give him his start in life. Giuseppe. Digli quel che mi hai detto.

GIUSEPPE. *(To VINNIE:)* E la tua, quella macchina li fuori?

VINNIE. *(Trying to follow:)* My car—?

BOSS. He's asking if that's your car outside.

VINNIE. Oh. Well, yeah.

(BOSS nods to GIUSEPPE.)

GIUSEPPE. Ho vista quella macchina nella strada hieri sera. Prima che Tommy sparisse. L'ho vista dalla finestra. Non ho visto chi guidava. Ma ho visto la macchina. Ho visto la targa.

BOSS. That's all, Giuseppe. You can go. Puoi andare. *(GUISEPPE goes.)* What were you doin' in the neighborhood today, Vinnie?

VINNIE. Me?

BOSS. He saw your car.

VINNIE. I musta been one that looked like mine.

BOSS. He saw the license plate number.

VINNIE. I wasn't ...

BOSS. Do you know anything about Tommy?

VINNIE. No.

(Beat.)

BOSS. I sense ... that you *do.*

VINNIE. No! I—

BOSS. Vinnie. Don't mess with me now.

VINNIE. Honest, Boss, I—

BOSS. What were you doing on this block, Vinnie?

VINNIE. I wasn't—! *(The BOSS starts to rise from his chair.)* — My *wife* was!

(Pause.)

BOSS. What?

VINNIE. My wife had the car today.

BOSS. Your wife?

VINNIE. Yeah.

(Beat.)

BOSS. What is this with your wife, Vinnie? You losing control of your wife?

VINNIE. No.

BOSS. Vinnie.

VINNIE. She's ... I dunno, Boss. She's gettin' kinda crazy a little.

BOSS. Crazy?

VINNIE. Kids. She's alla time obsessin' about havin' kids.

BOSS. Kids?

VINNIE. She wants to have a kid. She wants to have a kid so bad, she keeps takin' other peoples' kids home pretendin' that they're hers. Last week it was some shoppin' mall in New Jersey. She wants a kid, Boss.

BOSS. Maybe you should give her a child, Vinnie. Isn't that your responsibility? To give her a child?

VINNIE. Yeah. I dunno, Boss.

BOSS. I get ... I get an unsettling feeling, Vinnie. I don't like this feeling. I get an unsettling feeling that something has happened to my boy Tommy.

VINNIE. Something—?

BOSS. You *know* something. About my boy Tommy.

VINNIE. No. Well, my wife, see, she—

BOSS. Has your wife done something with my boy Tommy?

VINNIE. She—

BOSS. Vinnie! Answer me! Or I'll get Giuseppe in here to hold you down and I will personally slice your balls off!

(Beat.)

VINNIE. She took him.

BOSS. She—?

VINNIE. She took him home with her.

BOSS. Matta!

VINNIE. I know, I know, she *is* crazy! I told her—

BOSS. Stronza! Vai a prenderla! Is Tommy all right? Is he okay?

VINNIE. He's fine. She—I haven't actually seen him. She called me from a, a pay phone, they're out in New Jersey—

BOSS. New Jersey?

VINNIE. She's—look. She's kinda lost her mind, Boss. She thinks it's her kid! She's not gonna hurt him or anything. She just, like I said, she's just trying to be a mother, or, somethin', I dunno. It's this thing with her, she—

BOSS. Get my son back! Now! I'll send Vincente with you—

VINNIE. No! No, let me go alone. I'll, I'll go alone. *(Beat.)* She *trusts* me, Boss. Me, I can *talk* to her, I can *reason* with her, I can, I know I can get Tommy back for you. *(Beat.)* I *promise* it's gonna be okay, I swear it will. I'll go find her and I'll bring Tommy back to you.

(Beat.)

BOSS. Vinnie.

VINNIE. Yeah?

(BOSS rises, walks over to VINNIE. Reaches into his shoulder holster, hands him his own gun.)

BOSS. You take *care* of this problem. This is a problem and I want you to take care of it.
VINNIE. I—
BOSS. Do you understand what I'm *saying*?
VINNIE. Y—yes.
BOSS. Do you *understand*?

(Pause. Their eyes meet. This is clearly an order to VINNIE. VINNIE takes in what the BOSS has just said, then:)

VINNIE. Yes.

(Beat. BOSS steps back, looks VINNIE over, then nods.)

BOSS. Good. Soon ... soon you're gonna be part of this Family. I want to know that you're gonna take that serious. I got to know. I gotta know that I can depend on you.
VINNIE. Yes sir.
BOSS. Is that clear?
VINNIE. Yes!

(The BOSS goes back to his leather recliner chair, eases into it. Turns the lamp off again. It is semi-dark. VINNIE is still standing there, trying to figure out his options. Blackout.)

Scene 6

(SETTING: Later. Hospital corridor.
AT RISE: VINNIE standing. ANN-MARIE seated on a bench, crying.)

VINNIE. They *what*? *(She nods. Sobbing.)* Wait a minute, lemme get this straight here. *Who* came in—?
ANN-MARIE. Mrs. Hennicker.
VINNIE. Who?
ANN-MARIE. From Child Services.
VINNIE. What—?

ANN-MARIE. She had these two cops with her. They gave me these papers— *(She offers them to VINNIE, who stares at them, numbly.)* That doctor told 'em we was unfit parents or somethin'—

VINNIE. I knew that woman doctor was gonna be nothin' but trouble. I gotta go find her ...

ANN-MARIE. I tried; she already left.

VINNIE. What?

ANN-MARIE. She's off duty.

(VINNIE goes over to a wall-mounted pay phone, rips the phone book off its mount.)

VINNIE. What's her name again?

ANN-MARIE. McCaffrey.

VINNIE. McCaffrey ... *(Finds the page.)* Will ya lookit that? There are about a million McCaffrey's on this page! Don't those Irish ever stop breedin'? They're worse than rabbits!

ANN-MARIE. Mrs. Hennicker said—

VINNIE. Okay now, which one was this?

ANN-MARIE. From Child Services, she said—

VINNIE. She was the one with the two cops?

ANN-MARIE. Yeah.

VINNIE. Where'd they take him?

ANN-MARIE. She wouldn't tell me. THEY TOOK MY BABY!!!

VINNIE. Ann-Marie ... Ann-Marie! Will you can it for a minute? He wasn't your kid!

ANN-MARIE. *(Remembering this:)* Oh.

VINNIE. What did he say? Was he still talkin' or anything?

ANN-MARIE. No, that doctor gave him drugs so she could, could set his arm.

VINNIE. Woman doctor. I knew I couldn't trust *her.* So he was still sleepin' when they took him?

ANN-MARIE. Yeah.

VINNIE. Good.

(VINNIE looks at the forms.)

ANN-MARIE. What're you doing?

VINNIE. *(Reading:)* Mrs. T.M. Hennicker ... s'at what that looks like to you?

ANN-MARIE. Yeah.

VINNIE. *(Consults the phone book.)* Hennicker ... Hennicker ... here it is. T. M. Hennicker, 1211 Ocean Parkway. You got a quarter?

ANN-MARIE. A—?

VINNIE. Yeah, gimme a, gimme a quarter.

ANN-MARIE. I ain't got no change.

VINNIE. What, are you kiddin' me?

ANN-MARIE. We rushed outta the house so fast, I didn't have time to think.

VINNIE. Oh, excuse me, like you think when you *do* have time.

(VINNIE looks around, checks to see if anyone is watching. Takes out his gun, uses it as a hammer to bust open the pay phone coin box. Quarters and dimes stream out onto the floor. He catches a fistful, hands it to ANN-MARIE.)

ANN-MARIE. Oh, good! I needed change for the laundry.

(She dumps it all in her purse. Sees something in the purse, takes it out: nail polish. Time for a very quick touchup. VINNIE consults the phone book, drops a quarter into the phone, dials.)

VINNIE. Hello? Hell—? Is this Mrs. Hennicker? Is Mrs. Hennicker there? Well you go get her ass *up* then! *(Pause.)* Hello? Mrs. Hennicker? Yeah. You came down to the hospital awhile ago and you took a kid away from his screaming mother and I want him back. *(VINNIE indicates to ANN-MARIE that she should "make some noise." She begins to cry and sob, touching up her nails all the while.)* What? I can't he—? What? *(VINNIE motions to ANN-MARIE to "turn it down." She does.)* I wanna know where he *is.* Uh-huh ... well, you listen to me and you listen good: I know where you *live.* Okay? And if you don't tell me where the kid *is,* I'm gonna come over there and use your face for a brillo pad. *(Beat.)* Our what? Our Lady of ... where is that? Uh-huh. Okay. Good. I'm goin' over there now. And he'd better be there. Cause if he's *not* ... *(He's about to hang up, gets a last thought.)* And don't you even think of calling the cops 'cause if you *do* ... I swear to God, I'll kill you.

(He hangs up.)

VINNIE. Was that okay?

ANN-MARIE. Oh, Vinnie. You were great!

(She kisses him.)

VINNIE. Let's go then.

(Blackout.)

Scene 7

(SETTING: Later. ANN-MARIE and VINNIE stand on the front steps of the "Our Lady of Perpetual Shelter" Catholic Orphanage.
AT RISE: A NUN, in habit, blocks their entrance into the shelter. Far away, in the bowels of the shelter, we can hear a baby or two crying from time to time during the scene.)

NUN. ... I'm afraid that is out of the question.

VINNIE. Look, lady. I don't want no trouble.

NUN. Then leave. You look like a hoodlum, so leave.

VINNIE. We want our kid back!

NUN. Then I suggest you follow the proper judicial procedures and await the judgement of the State.

VINNIE. No, see, we don't have *time* for all that crap.

NUN. In God's kingdom there *is* no time.

VINNIE. Well, I dunno about God, but I gotta have this kid home by midnight.

NUN. The Orphanage is closed.

VINNIE. Look, I don't wanna hafta hurt you, lady, but—

NUN. *(Firm and accusatory:)* Are you Catholic?

VINNIE. *(Frightened, all those memories of Catholic school coming back:)* Ma'am—?

NUN. Are you a good Catholic boy?

ANN-MARIE. I wouldn't call him "good."

VINNIE. Shuttup!

NUN. Shame on you! You know better than this! You were brought up to behave better than this! Slipping around in the dark of night like some insect. Hiding in the shadows. Threatening nuns. Abusing your child!

VINNIE. I never abused him!

NUN. I want you to say three Hail Mary's and go home to pray for your soul.

VINNIE. And I want you to get the hell outta the way so's we can find the kid!

NUN. And if I don't? Eh? What're you going to do? Hit me? Kill me?

VINNIE. Maybe.

NUN. You will be damned straight to hell.

VINNIE. I already am!

NUN. I am not afraid of you.

VINNIE. Well, you oughtta be.

NUN. *(Turning to go inside.)* Goodnight.

ANN-MARIE. WAIT!!! *(Something in ANN-MARIE's voice sounds so urgent, so heartfelt, so heart-broken, that it makes the NUN stop. ANN-MARIE steps up to the NUN, all humble, quiet and very still. No pretense.)* I'm going to tell you the truth.

VINNIE. *(Worried:)* Ann-Marie!

(ANN-MARIE motions for VINNIE to be quiet. He obeys.)

ANN-MARIE. This is not our kid. *(VINNIE deflates, throws up his hands in defeat. The NUN listens.)* We're taking care of him. See, his parents are visitin' from Florida and they're sittin' at home right now callin' the Police, the F.B.I., the N.R.A., the TV stations, the dairies—

NUN. Dairies—?

ANN-MARIE. Yeah! To get his *picture* on the back a the milk cartons! Anything they can *think* of! They want him back so bad they're goin' crazy and growin' ulcers! *(She steps forward even more and makes particular emphasis with this:)* They *trusted* us. Do you know what that *means*? They put the life of their child in our hands. They trusted us. And we failed them. Now, no matter what, they will never trust anybody else with their child again. Not ever. They're sitting at home, hunched over the phone right now in the glow of the TV set calling anybody they can think of. Anybody. Total strangers, even. And *us*—their closest family ... we let them *down. (Silence. ANN-MARIE bows her head in shame and humility. The NUN is moved. VINNIE is amazed.)* To say we learned a lesson is like sayin' there's no whores in the Vatican. *(The NUN is shocked. ANN-MARIE tries to regain ground from this slip:)*—but we *have* learned our lesson. And all we want to do right now is make this right. *Please* help us make this right. Please let us take him. Take him back to the loving arms of his parents. They're worried sick about him. They're ...

(She starts to cry, cannot go on. She throws herself in VINNIE's arms. VINNIE embraces her, holds her. The NUN wipes a tear away.)

NUN. I'll go get him.

(Blackout.)

Scene 8

(SETTING: A few moments later. VINNIE's car.
AT RISE: The KID is out cold on the back seat. VINNIE drives. Si-
lence.)

VINNIE. He okay?

(ANN-MARIE glances back.)

ANN-MARIE. He's still sleeping.
VINNIE. What time is it?
ANN-MARIE. 11:15.
VINNIE. *(Sigh of relief:)* Thank God! Talk about by the skin a
your butt! *(Beat. VINNIE smiles.)* Hey. You were really terrific back
there.
ANN-MARIE. I was?
VINNIE. Yeah. *(Laughs remembering it.)* You was! Where'd you
get that story from?
ANN-MARIE. I dunno. I just thought it up, I guess.
VINNIE. Hah! Well you did good.
ANN-MARIE. Thanks.
VINNIE. I was proud a you.
ANN-MARIE. Thank you, Vinnie.

(She scoots over on the seat closer to him and cuddles. He puts his
arm around her. They drive in silence a moment.)

ANN-MARIE. Hey.
VINNIE. Hmm?
ANN-MARIE. You never told me what happened ...
VINNIE. Happened?
ANN-MARIE. You know. *(He doesn't.)* When you went to see
the Boss.
VINNIE. *(Who has forgotten all about this until now:)* Oh.
ANN-MARIE. What'd he say?
VINNIE. *(Removing his arm:)* Nothin'.
ANN-MARIE. Did you see him?
VINNIE. Ah ... yeah.
ANN-MARIE. So. What'd he say?

VINNIE. Nothin'! Get off my back, willya?

ANN-MARIE. I'm just askin'!

VINNIE. You're always "just askin'."

ANN-MARIE. What're you gettin' so pissed about all of a sudden?

VINNIE. Nothin'!

ANN-MARIE. You oughtta be happy, I got your ass outta a swing!

VINNIE. Sling.

ANN-MARIE. Whatever. You oughtta be happy!

VINNIE. I'm happy, I'm happy!

(Beat.)

ANN-MARIE. Everything's okay, right?

VINNIE. *(No:)* Yeah ...

ANN-MARIE. The Boss is gettin' his kid back ...

VINNIE. Yeah ...

ANN-MARIE. You're gettin' made ...

VINNIE. Yeah ...

(She senses a problem.)

ANN-MARIE. Vinnie, what's wrong? Something is wrong.

VINNIE. Nothing is wrong! It's just ...

(VINNIE pulls over, stops the car. Takes a moment to gather his thoughts.)

ANN-MARIE. What?

(VINNIE tries hard to find the words to explain this; it must be obvious that down in the very center of his being, VINNIE is wrestling with the biggest problem of his life.)

VINNIE. When I was a kid, my dad used to beat the crap outta my ma. And me. Only time we ever had a break was when he got locked up every once and awhile for startin' a fight or somethin'. And, for a night or two, my ma and me'd have some peace and quiet. She'd hold me ... talk to me ... sing me to sleep ... *(Beat.)* That was my only peace. Then one day he came home while she was ironing his shirts and he hit her with the iron. He killed her. I could not understand that. How he could destroy the only good thing in my life. He went to the Pen and died there. I went to live in an orphanage. All my life...

I've wanted to be part of a family. That's why being Made is such a big deal, Ann-Marie. It means I'm gonna be part of a Family.

ANN-MARIE. Vinnie, we can start our *own* family.

VINNIE. Ann-Marie ... my ma was gone just like that. *(He snaps his fingers.)* What if somethin' happened to you? I'd be all alone again. You see what I'm sayin'? *(She doesn't.)* You can't trust people to be there. No matter how much you want to, you can't. That's why the Family is so important to me. See, it don't ever go away. Or change. Or die. It's always there for you. You do what the Boss tells you, you're okay. You're taken care of. Like a kid, y'know? *But. You gotta do* 'xactly what he tells ya.

(VINNIE reaches into his jacket, takes out his gun. He is fighting back tears, his hand shaking like a leaf.)

ANN-MARIE. Vinnie—?
VINNIE. Ann-Marie, I love you ...
ANN-MARIE. Vinnie! What're you—?
VINNIE. *(Crying:)* I'm so sorry!
ANN-MARIE. What're you—? What—? Vinnie! VINNIE!!!

(Blackout.)

Scene 9

(SETTING: After midnight. Outside the BOSS's front door. Crickets chirping.
AT RISE: It is dark. A light above the door comes on. The BOSS opens the door. He is wearing a bathrobe.)

BOSS. Vinnie?
VINNIE. Hey, Boss.
BOSS. What're you doin' out here? It's after midnight.
VINNIE. You told me, be back here by 12.
BOSS. Oh.
VINNIE So I'm back! Listen: I got somethin' for you—
BOSS. —Not now, Vinnie.
VINNIE. —out on the back seat.
BOSS. It's late.
VINNIE. I got your *kid*, Boss!

(Beat.)

BOSS. My *kid*?
VINNIE. Yeah.
BOSS. Tommy?
VINNIE. Yeah!
BOSS. You got my kid?
VINNIE. Yeah!
BOSS. *You* got my *kid*?
VINNIE. Yeah!
BOSS. No you don't.
VINNIE. I do; come look—
BOSS. Vinnie, we found *my* kid.

(Silence, except for the crickets.)

VINNIE. What?
BOSS. Coupla hours ago.
VINNIE. Who did?
BOSS. Eddie "Ear Lobes" Vinetti.
VINNIE. Eddie "Ear Lobes" found your kid?
BOSS. Yeah. It was no big deal, really. He was spendin' the night over at his friend Billy Franco's house. He forgot to tell us! He was safe and sound the whole time, I just didn't know it! It's fine, Vinnie. Everything's all fine now. Go home and get some sleep. It's all fine. *(Beat.)* Vinnie. You okay?
VINNIE. No.
BOSS. What's a matter?
VINNIE. A matter?
BOSS. Yeah.
VINNIE. I got a kid in my back *seat*, I thought he was *yours*!
BOSS. Where?
VINNIE. Right there!

(VINNIE hands the BOSS a flashlight. The BOSS leaves the stage. Pause. VINNIE paces miserably under the porch light. After a few moments, the BOSS returns.)

BOSS. He's one a the neighborhood kids.
VINNIE. What?
BOSS. One a these rug rats, lives around here. I dunno which one. I seen him around.
VINNIE. It's Tommy!

BOSS. It's not Tommy! Vinnie, it don't look nothin' like Tommy! *(Beat.)* 'Course, you ain't seen him in a coupla years. They grow up fast ...

VINNIE. Wait. So you got Tommy back?

BOSS. Idn't that what I said? What you, need me to go to the Pathmark and get some Q-Tips for you? Yeah. We got Tommy. I gotta go to bed. Goodnight.

(The BOSS starts to go.)

VINNIE. So ... what do I do with *this* kid?

BOSS. I dunno. Stick him in the bushes someplace. Up there. He'll find his way home. *(BOSS starts to go again, stops.)* Hey. Tomorrow night. Big night, Vinnie? Eh?

(BOSS chuckles, goes inside, leaving VINNIE standing alone, completely shattered, under the porch light. Blackout.)

Scene 10

(SETTING: Friday. The upscale men's clothing store from Scene 1. AT RISE: VINNIE is standing before the mirror, wearing his newly-tailored suit. CHARLES stands nearby, waiting to be of service. A long, long pause. VINNIE's eyes just look absolutely dead.)

CHARLES. Ahem.

VINNIE. *(Croaked voice, awakened from his daze:)* Yeah?

CHARLES. Is everything all right, sir?

(Pause. VINNIE looks at CHARLES, has to focus. It's almost as if he doesn't know who CHARLES is.)

VINNIE. What?

CHARLES. Is everything all right?

(Beat.)

VINNIE. Yeah.

CHARLES. Will there be anything else then?

(VINNIE looks around, as if for something to latch onto, grab onto, to make things familiar again. Pause. He looks helplessly at CHARLES.)

VINNIE. No.

(Blackout.)

Scene 11

(SETTING: Friday night. The BOSS's basement.
AT RISE: The stage is black. A match is lit. It, in turn, lights a Holy Card, which begins to burn. As it does, the stage is illuminated somewhat and we can see that we are in the BOSS's basement. The BOSS holds the burning Holy Card up in the air. We are in the middle of a ceremony. VINNIE is Getting Made. In front of the BOSS, back to the audience, stands VINNIE. Upstage, behind the BOSS, are several Mafiosi. The BOSS hands the card to one of the men, who in turn hands it to another, then another. The last to receive the card is VINNIE. The BOSS motions for him to come closer. VINNIE does.)

BOSS. *(An oath:)* Come si bruscia questa santa cosi si brucera la mia anima.
VINNIE. Come si bruscia questa santa cosi si brucera la mia anima.

(VINNIE holds the burning card, staring at the flame, repeating the oath mechanically. As he finishes speaking the BOSS holds an ashtray out for VINNIE to drop the burning card into. VINNIE does. The MEN applaud. Somebody turns the lights on and the gathering becomes more informal. There is chatting and patter in the background as each man walks up to VINNIE, kisses him once on each cheek, hugs him, and ad-libs a "Welcome to the Family." VINNIE just stands there, rigid, all this sort of happening around him, as if he is in a dream and not totally present. In the background, as all this happens, we hear:)

MAN 1. Hey Billy.
MAN 2. Yeah?
MAN 1. You finally got some a them cards without the *plastic* on 'em!

(Laughter from the others.)

    MAN 2. I hadda go to 15 different funeral homes to find 'em.
    MAN 3. Who had 'em?
    MAN 2. Eh?
    MAN 3. Where'd you finally find 'em?
    MAN 2. Scalpini's.
    MAN 1. Oh, out in Carroll Gardens?
    MAN 2. Yeah, that's the one.
    MAN 1. I know him, yeah. One time he did some work for me.
    BOSS. I remember when we made Harry Vinolli, we had them cards with the plastic on 'em. I couldn't get 'em to light no matter *what* I did. I think we ended up burnin' somebody's Lotto ticket or somethin'.
    MAN 2. I think it was my Lotto ticket you burned. And I probably had the winnin' number!

(Laughter. All the men have "greeted" VINNIE into the fold and have stepped Upstage, out of the way. All except the BOSS, who now approaches VINNIE.)

    BOSS. Vinnie. My boy ...

(It seems as if a coil wound tight, deep inside of VINNIE, is about to spring loose. The BOSS approaches him, kisses him on both cheeks. VINNIE is visibly quaking all over.)

    BOSS. Welcome to the Family.

(VINNIE bursts into angry, helpless tears. The Wiseguys naturally just assume that he's moved by the Ceremony and they break out into applause. VINNIE grabs the BOSS's lapels and thrusts his face into the BOSS's chest sobbing. Applause continues as lights begin a slow fade. The BOSS looks down at VINNIE and somehow perceives his misery. VINNIE continues to sob into the BOSS's chest from deep within his soul as lights fade out. Blackout.)

END OF PLAY

FAMILY VALUES PROPERTY PLOT

Scene 1
tailor's mirror
chair
magazine
box of straight pins
large dictionary
wad of bills (Vinnie)

Scene 2
suggestion of car w/
  steering wheel
dictionary

Scene 3
bed
bedside table
damp cloth
telephone
dictionary

Scene 4
hospital bed
chair
other hospital
  room equipment &
  furniture (optional)
dictionary
clipboard (McCaffrey)
stethescope (McCaffrey)
ammonia capsules
3 pagers (Ann-Marie,
  Vinnie, McCaffrey)
syringe

Scene 5
leather recliner
end table
practical table lamp
additional chair

Scene 6
pay phone
bench
phone book
release forms
coins
nail polish (Ann-Marie)

Scene 7
doorway w/orphanage
  signage

Scene 8
car (same as Scene 2)

Scene 9
Boss's doorway
  w/porch light
flashlight

Scene 10
Same as Scene 1

Scene 11
pack or box of matches
Holy Card
ash tray
candles (optional)

FAMILY VALUES COSTUME PLOT

VINNIE
Scene 1
unfinished suit for fitting
shoulder holster & gun
additional dress slacks
Scenes 2-9
leather sportcoat
gold chains
slacks from Scene 1
shoulder holster & gun
Scenes 10, 11
finished suit from Scene 1

ANN-MARIE
Scenes 1 - 8
tight-fitting slacks &
  blouse (or dress w/short
  skirt)
high heels
purse

CHARLES
Scenes 1 & 10
fine tailored suit

THE KID
Scenes 3,4
play clothes
Scene 8
add cast on arm

DR. McCAFFREY
Scene 4
scrub suit or white
  doctor's coat
hospital I.D. badge

THE BOSS
Scene 5
dark suit
dark shirt
Scene 9
bathrobe
Scene 11
same as Scene 5, add dark tie

GUISEPPE
Scene 5
dark suit
dark shirt

THE NUN
Scene 7
full habit

MAFIOSI
Scene 11
dark suits w/shirts and ties

www.ingramcontent.com/pod-product-compliance
Lightning Source LLC
Chambersburg PA
CBHW070613120726
47909CB00004B/1204